MAGIC UNITED

MAGIC UNITED

THE WITCHES OF PRESSLER STREET™ BOOK FIVE

MARTHA CARR

MICHAEL ANDERLE

LMBPN Publishing
PMB 196, 2540 South Maryland Pkwy
Las Vegas, NV 89109

First US edition, March 2020
Version 1.02, February 2021
eBook ISBN: 978-1-64202-791-4
Print ISBN: 978-1-64202-792-1

THE MAGIC UNITED TEAM

To the Early Readers Team
Kathleen Fettig
Michael Robbins
Debi Sateren
Michael Baumann

Special shout out to Grace Snokes, Lynne Stiegler, Judah Raine, Kelly O'Donnell and Stephen Campbell for their general badassery behind the scenes to keep everything running so smoothly.

From Martha

To all those who love to read, and like a good puzzle inside
a good story
To Michael Anderle for his generosity
to all his fellow authors
To Louie and Jackie
And in memory of my big sister,
Dr. Diana Deane Carr
who first taught me about magic, Star Trek,
DC Comics and flaming cherries jubilee

From Michael

To Family, Friends and
Those Who Love
To Read.
May We All Enjoy Grace
To Live The Life We Are
Called.

CHAPTER ONE

In Laura Hadstrom's bedroom in the house on Pressler Street, Nickie and Emily Hadstrom darted out of their sister's walk-in closet and stumbled across the carpeted floor toward the bed. Nathan leapt out after them, slammed the door shut, and pressed his full weight against it. A loud, chuffing grunt came from inside the closet, followed by a few panicked squawks and a sound like a cross between a laughing hyena and a braying mule. Something thumped against the door, rattling the doorknob and bumping the part-Kashgar a few inches off the wood.

"Grab something to jam under the handle," Nathan muttered.

"Uh…" Emily glanced at Nickie, then quickly searched her oldest sister's bedroom. "Everything we would've been able to use for that is actually *in* her closet."

"Just look." The door thumped and trembled behind Nathan again. He gritted his teeth and tried not to let the soles of his sneakers slip away beneath him across the hardwood floor.

Both Hadstrom sisters whirled in opposite directions, checking the meticulously placed items on Laura's desk, looking under the bed, peeking quickly into the bathroom. Emily scratched her head. "Everything Laura cares about is in that room with all the creatures—"

A series of grating, desperate scratches came from the other side of the closet door. One of the beasts in Laura Hadstrom's walk-in closet-turned-artifact-museum-and-magical menagerie let out a vicious roar. Another shrieked —or the same one, for all they knew—and Nathan struggled against another few thumps. "Just find something!"

"Hey, it's not like physical barricades are her preferred method of defense," Nickie shouted back. She ran a hand through her long dark hair, shared by all the Hadstrom sisters, and grabbed the office chair behind her older sister's desk. "Will this work?"

By the time she wheeled it over to the closet, it was all too clear that Laura preferred her office chairs low to the ground. Nickie tried to prop it up under the doorknob as Nathan braced his body against the wood, but the wheels made a good chair-jamming pretty impossible.

"Just forget it." Nathan grunted. "Either of you have any idea how long it'll take those things to give up?"

The Hadstrom sisters exchanged glances and shook their heads. "Nickie sang one of them into a trance earlier," Emily said with a shrug.

"Em, I don't think singing through a closed door to a bunch of panicked magical creatures that are out of their cages is gonna do anything."

"Fair enough."

"Sang it into a trance, huh?" Nathan scoffed and braced

himself for another thump at his back that hadn't come yet. "Bet it was one of those tiny things in the water, huh?"

"Nope." Emily folded her arms. "It was the gorlek."

Nathan blinked. "Seriously?"

"Trust me," Nickie said. "I was just as surprised."

"They're not supposed to be that big." Nathan shook his head and let out a chuckle of disbelief. "I can't believe she *has* one. Right here in her…closet."

"Yeah, it's a little weird that that's where she hides all her secrets." Emily rubbed her palms on the legs of her jeans and shook out her hands. "Actually, for Laura, maybe that's not so weird at all."

"Apparently, it wasn't that big last week," Nickie added.

"But magic's been upping the stakes by the day." Nathan nodded in understanding, then straightened against the door and stared at the ceiling as the sounds of crazed animals inside Laura's magically enlarged secret lair faded behind him. "She uses magic to keep all those things in their pens?"

"Yep." Emily snapped her fingers, waiting for even a glimmer of light to flash from the copper legacy ring on her thumb. Nothing. "Something about 'regulating the habitats' too."

"I bet that's why they're out." Nathan stepped slowly away from the door, as if any of the beasts could see him testing the waters and sighed. "Sounds like they're figuring out how to settle down."

Wrinkling her nose, Nickie softly rolled the office chair back behind her big sister's desk and lifted her hands. With magic getting unpredictable and more impossible to control by the hour, it didn't seem that far out of the question that what looked like a normal office chair could become as dangerous as the thing that had kidnapped Laura. "You know, I'd say we should keep this little issue to ourselves."

"*That's* not gonna happen." Emily snorted. "Laura would notice a clear bowl turned just a tiny bit. That place is a mess."

"She's gonna be pissed, huh?" Nathan ran a hand through his hair and shot a dubious glance at the closet door.

"Under any other circumstances, Nathan, I'd say that's a yes." Nickie spread her arms. "But Laura's been kidnapped by a gorafrex and taken who knows where and magic is broken, so what other choice do we have?"

"The longest grudge she held against me was…what? Maybe a month?"

Nickie shot her little sister a knowing look. "It was more like two, Em."

For a few seconds, Emily managed to pull off her completely-clueless-innocence face, eyes wide and unblinking. When the Hadstrom sisters were kids, her lower lip had trembled when she made that face, but she just couldn't bring herself to do it this time. "Okay, fine. Maybe it *was* two months. Maybe if she'd told me that beat-up can was actually for ceremonial purposes, I wouldn't have poured bacon grease into it."

Choosing to ignore how weird all of that sounded, Nathan rubbed a hand over his mouth and chin. "So, I'm in for two months of Laura not talking to me?"

"Definitely not. Like Nickie said, special circumstances and everything. I'd give it more like two weeks." Emily nodded toward the closet door. "Which is probably how long it'll take her to put everything back together in there."

Nathan took that bit of disheartening news like a champ. "Maybe not if she lets me help."

Emily raised her eyebrows and turned away to search her oldest sister's room. "Good luck with that."

"Did you guys see anything in there like what we're looking for?" Nickie pulled back the comforter of Laura's king-sized bed, shrugged, then figured she might as well check under the mattress too.

"Sorry," Nathan said, stepping into the bathroom to look through the neatly stacked towels on the rack beside the tub. "I was a little busy trying not to get ripped to shreds by those… Are they *dragons*?"

"Scratchhok, I think."

Emily opened the drawers of her sister's desk and rifled through the neat boxes of pens and color-coordinated paperclips in one, the stacks of perfectly aligned paper in another, and the file folder in a bottom drawer that had only two files in it, labeled Utilities and Rent. She quickly closed the drawers and thought about opening Laura's laptop before reconsidering. *Can't put a digital file into a Tibetan singing bowl to track magical frequencies.*

Nathan stepped out of the bathroom again and leaned against the doorframe. "And she just keeps all those animals in there because…"

"Because she likes to collect things," Emily said. "Because she has this weird inability to see anybody or anything struggle and just has to help them."

"I wouldn't call that weird. Kind of endearing, actually."

"Oh, yeah? Is that what you were thinking when we

were running away from a giant slug that breathes fire in her closet?" The youngest Hadstrom sister looked up at the physics professor, then frowned. "Were you just looking through her bathroom stuff?"

Nickie crawled backward from where she'd stuck her head under Laura's bed, pushed herself to her knees, and turned around to look at Nathan with a mocking smile. "Why the *bathroom?*"

"What?" Nathan spread his arms and glanced at them. "It's not out of the question. I thought… I mean…"

"You thought all women keep their important personal items in the bathroom?" Emily stuck a hand on her hip. "Like makeup and hair products and lotion? Stuff like that?"

"Woah. No. I just meant—"

"Hate to break it to you, Nate, but if you think Laura spends more time in the bathroom than—I dunno, *cooking* —you don't know her as well as you think you do."

Nathan lifted his hands in surrender and pressed his lips together. "I wasn't trying to start a thing."

"Em." Nickie pushed herself up to her feet and pulled open the drawer of Laura's bedside table. "Give him a break, huh?"

Emily snorted. "Yeah, I'm just messin' with you, man. That was pretty good thinking, actually."

He laughed when she pointed at him before turning to open the final drawer in Laura's desk.

"That's the last place most people would think to look if we're talking about artifacts or anything super-important to a Hadstrom witch. But Laura would be too freaked out about leaving anything valuable in the place where she takes a shower."

"Uh-oh." Nathan pulled a jokingly hesitant face. "What does she have against showers?"

"What?"

Nickie shook her head. "She put up climate-control charms around the creature pens in her closet and something else that dusts and sweeps and mops up for her in there. And she's an archaeologist."

"Steam, soap, and random things floating through the air around something Laura's particularly attached to?" Emily scoffed. "No way."

"Right." Nathan stepped farther into the bedroom, then stuck his thumb behind him. "Can't use her toothbrush or anything?"

"Yeah, that worked with Dave," Nickie said, squinting at the room as she tried to find something else to search through. "And the gorafrex was using his Peabrain magic at that point, anyway. Dave hadn't had a chance yet to make any magical connections with anything."

"We're following magical frequencies *and* the personal value of whatever we're supposed to find," Emily added. Then she pulled two rolls of stamps out of the last drawer, followed by one of those four-foot ropes of red licorice still in the clear plastic wrapper. "I don't know if she's had this since before Grandma died or she keeps a private stash."

When the end of the licorice rope thumped to the floor, Nickie let out a sharp laugh. "Not what we're looking for, Em."

Nathan shot another glance at the closed closet door and cocked his head. "Where does she keep her clothes?"

"Dresser," the Hadstrom sisters answered together without looking at him.

Emily stepped back from the desk and put her hands on her hips. "You know, given how much trouble she went through putting up the wards around her room and hiding all her stuff, you'd think she'd have an even better protected spot that just screams, 'Property of Laura Hadstrom. Keep out.'"

She scanned the top of the desk again, then lifted her gaze toward all the framed awards, degrees, and certifications mounted on the wall. "I mean, there's gotta be something that—oh." Emily's eyes widened, and she spun to grin at Nickie. "Hey, remember when Laura got so bent out of shape at my graduation?"

Nickie puffed out a dismissive breath and dropped a navy-blue sleeping mask back into the nightstand drawer. "Because you didn't wanna go back inside to find your funny hat with the dangling string of achievement on the side? We should've known something was up just by how much she overreacted."

"I think I found what we need."

Nathan and Nickie both turned to see Emily pointing with an outstretched arm at one of the frames on the wall. Nickie ran a hand through her hair and grinned. "I think you're right, Em."

"I'm not sure which part's throwin' me off, here," Nathan muttered. "The fact that you guys think *that's* one of Laura's most valued possessions, or that your sister framed her cap and gown."

Emily wiggled her eyebrows. "It's *symbolic*. That's what she told me when I graduated. That I should go back and find the stupid cap because I might want to frame it someday. You know what? Throwing that stupid thing was pretty symbolic too. It meant, 'I'm done.'"

"Yep." Nickie laced her fingers and bent them back to crack her knuckles, then shook out her hands. "And short of her family and protecting innocent creatures she finds in the weirdest places, there's nothing more important to Laura than her success in school and her tenure and her career."

"Nothing." Emily shot Nathan a wink.

"Huh."

Nickie approached her sister in front of the desk. "Can you imagine her standing on top of this thing to hang all these up here?"

"Come on. She wouldn't be able to reach that high even if she *did* stand on the desk."

"That's what I thought. Magic put 'em up there. How much you wanna bet magic has to take 'em down?"

Emily shot her sister a sidelong glance. "You can't make a bet when the other person agrees with you."

"Still." Nickie shook out her hands again and glanced at the black legacy ring on her thumb. "Magic didn't work for us in Laura's closeted zoo."

Nathan pointed at her. "Hey, I said I was sorry."

"We know." Emily patted his shoulder with a reassuring nod. "I'm not a huge fan of the tiny leathery birds with razor-sharp talons, either. Especially their beaks." She lifted her hand to show him the small red mark on her index finger. "Even their *babies* got bite."

Nickie chuckled and stared at the framed cap and gown from Laura's graduation as a twenty-two-year-old doctoral candidate four years ago. "So, it'd be super-great if magic decided to work now."

"I'll sit this one out." Emily nodded.

With a deep breath, Nickie focused her attention on the clear glass within the simple black frame and raised her hand. It wasn't hard to think about her intention with magic, but for the last few days, *intending* to cast any kind of spell hadn't been enough to get the job done. *At least help us figure out what kind of wards she put on this thing.*

The black legacy ring on her thumb blinked with a soft silver light, which quickly sputtered out. Nickie tried again and reached farther toward the frame.

"You got this."

"Thanks, Em. Just trying to focus." The tingle of her witch's magic pulsed into Nickie's hand, but it wouldn't release. Or it wasn't working in the first place. The legacy ring grew warm on her finger, and sparks of blue light burst from the band in a small arc, trickling down around her hand like wilting flowers—and that was it. "Okay, I don't get mad very often. But I'm almost there right now."

"Just don't push it too hard, okay?" Emily studied her sister's clenched jaw and deeply furrowed brow.

"Maybe I should go get my wand."

"Nope. If the legacy rings aren't working, wands definitely won't. I'm gonna go see if I have any more of those revealing potions left, 'kay?" The minute Emily set her hand on her sister's shoulder, both their legacy rings flared to life. A brilliant thread of white light burst from each of them and streaked toward the frame on the bedroom wall.

The spell crackled around the clear glass, and with a splintering crack, the glass shattered and spilled all over Laura's desk. A few shards toppled to the floor and bounced in a growing pile of fragments. Then Laura's cap and gown tumbled one right after the other from their place in the frame and thumped onto the mess the Hadstrom sisters had made.

Emily slowly lifted her hand from Nickie's shoulder and stared at the shattered glass, her mouth hanging open. Nickie's arm was still outstretched toward the wall.

"Guess you just needed a little boost," Nathan remarked.

"How is that even a thing?" Stunned, Emily gazed down at her hand like she had no idea what it was. Her copper legacy ring didn't give her any answers, though.

"Well, okay." Blinking away her surprise, Nickie leaned over the desk and grabbed Laura's cap and gown. A whole new wave of shattered glass tinkled around the desk and onto the floor when she gently shook out the garments. She hastily folded the gown into her arms and nodded. "Find Laura first, clean up later."

She headed toward the bedroom door, and Nathan followed closely behind her.

Emily still stared at her hand. "Did we just figure out how to make magic work for us again?"

"Probably. Come on, Em! We can test it on the way."

CHAPTER TWO

"Okay, we got everything?" With the cap and gown tucked under her arm, Nickie glanced over the assortment of potions vials Emily had laid out on their long dining room table.

Pointing at each of the vials, Emily finished her mental tally, then quickly stuffed them back into the folds of the apron in which she'd been storing them. "Yeah, we're good. And…" She reached out to snatch the singing bowl by the rim with one hand and grunted at its weight.

"Then let's go." Nickie turned toward the foyer and the front door, glancing quickly back at Nathan. "You can totally stay here if you want. I don't know how long this'll take, but when we find her, we'll give you a call."

Emily brushed past the physics professor holding the singing bowl. She nudged him with her elbow and shot him a grin. "Shouldn't take too long. Couple hours at the most."

Nickie opened the front door, and Nathan scoffed. "Yeah, nice try."

Before Emily could close the front door behind her, Nathan pulled it open again and stepped out onto the landing. "I'm coming with you guys."

Emily blinked and watched him shut the door. "We appreciate the enthusiasm, man. We really do. But this is on us."

"Not a very convincing argument, Em." With a pert, humorless smile, Nathan stepped past the youngest Hadstrom sister and moved quickly down the walkway with his long stride.

"Seriously, though." Hiking the bowl up under her arm, Emily hurried down the walkway. Nathan and Nickie were already at the bottom of the concrete steps set into the hillside. "Nickie and I are the only ones who can do this. That's the whole 'Hadstrom legacy' part. And we all know there's no possibility you have Hadstrom blood in you."

"Creepy thought, Em." Nickie rounded the front of her car and stopped in front of the driver's side door to shoot Nathan a quick glance. "But she's right. Sorry, Nathan."

He stood perfectly still, eyes narrowed, as Emily leapt down the last stair and headed across the sidewalk toward the passenger's side door. "She said we'd call you when we find Laura, and that's a promise. Don't worry. We got this." She opened the door and slid into the passenger seat with a sigh. "Time to go."

Nickie started the engine, then glanced at the Tibetan singing bowl in her sister's lap. "Here." She handed over the cap and gown and buckled her seatbelt. "Just stuff it in there, I guess, and we'll see what happens."

The back door behind Emily opened swiftly, the car rocked a little with added weight, and then the door clicked shut again. Both sisters turned around in their seats to stare at Nathan. "You heard what we said, right?" Emily asked.

"Yep." Nathan strapped himself in and readjusted in the back seat. "Heard it loud and clear. And you're right. The gorafrex can only be captured and imprisoned by Hadstrom descendants with those rings. But I'm pretty sure that doesn't extend to rescuing one of *them*."

Nickie and Emily exchanged glances, and the youngest witch shrugged. "He's arguing semantics with us."

"Sure is."

Emily turned back toward the physics professor again. "I'm guessing a please and thank you won't get you out of the back seat, huh?"

Nathan pressed his lips together and shook his head. "Not even with a cherry on top."

With a sigh, Emily sat back in her seat and stared through the windshield. "How mad is Laura gonna be when she realizes we let someone else help us rescue her?"

"On a scale of one to ten?" Nickie tilted her head back and forth. "I'd give it a six. Six-point-five, maybe."

"I'm coming with you guys no matter what, so you don't have to spend any more time trying to convince me not to. It won't happen." Nathan pressed his hands against the edge of the back seat and leaned forward. "If it helps, I'm doing this for Laura *and* because this town and all the magicals in it are gonna start destroying each other if magic doesn't start acting the way it's supposed to. Which you need Laura to do, as the Hadstrom witches with those rings. If we had time, I'd make a few calls and bring a lot more people. She can be as mad as she wants after we get her away from that thing. I really don't care."

"Yeah, neither do we." Nickie tossed the thick waves of her hair back over her shoulder and nodded at her sister. "Fire it up, Em."

"Okay." Emily balled up Laura's graduation gown and started stuffing it into the singing bowl in her lap. The fabric gave her a little resistance at first, but then the rest of it slid right in as if she'd tossed it into a giant bucket. Then she lifted the wide, square cap with the dangling tassel and turned it back and forth over the bowl. "You think there's a best angle for this one?"

"I dunno, Em. Fold the thing if you have to."

"Yeah, I know it's to find Laura and rescue her, but if she pulls a bent and folded cap out of this bowl later…"

"It's not rocket science."

The physics professor in the back seat snorted.

"Okay, fine." Emily stuck one corner of the cap into the opening of the singing bowl. It was much too big for it. "Come on. I really don't wanna have to—"

The cap shrank in her hand, slipping out of her fingers and right into the bowl where she wanted it. It looked a quarter of its size resting there on top of the bunched-up gown. Emily leaned over the bowl and grinned. "That never gets old."

"And now we wait for the magical tracker to kick in."

Emily picked up the felt-covered mallet sitting on the seat beside her and drew it around and around the edge of the bowl. A low, smooth tone filled the car, wavering a little and making Nickie's ears buzz.

She stared at the bowl, drumming her fingers on the

steering wheel. Then she paused and turned quickly toward Nathan again. "You can help us get her out of...wherever the gorafrex took her. Maybe having an extra pair of magical hands will come in useful. If you can get magic to work at all. Who knows? But that's under one condition."

"Anything, Nickie." Nathan nodded, his eyes wide and letting off that very faint hint of a violet glow.

"Don't try to fight that thing, okay? The last guy who thought he could take down the gorafrex was not a Hadstrom witch either, and it almost got him killed. Plus, I had to do a *lot* of emergency healing to save a Peabrain's life after the fact. Which was really lucky, because magic had pretty messed up our whole plans that day."

"Help but don't fight the stowaway creature on this ship hunting wizards and witches for blood magic. Got it."

"She's serious, Nate." Emily didn't take her eyes off the singing bowl, watching intently for the first flash of colored light that would show them where to head next. "We have to keep this whole thing on the down-low just so all of Austin doesn't freak out about a witch-killer on the loose. You know because you've already helped us and Laura likes you."

"I'm glad you mentioned that part." A smile twitched at the corner of Nathan's lips. "Would a Kashgar vow make either of you feel any better?"

"Not really."

"Just a promise from you," Emily added. "We have to trust you not to jump in and try to save the day. Because we all know that won't work."

"I can follow orders." Nodding, Nathan sat back in his seat again. "I won't touch the gorafrex. But I can help."

"Cool. Glad we're on the same page." Emily frowned at the singing bowl, which hadn't let out so much as a flash or a tiny spark of magic. Lifting the mallet, she flicked the side of the bowl a few times, bringing out a muted ring. "What's taking this thing so long?"

"Two and a half powered energy cores, Em. Magic being torn apart from the inside out. Remember?"

Emily huffed in irritation. "Would've been nice of the Engineers to consider all the possibilities before they built an escape pod in a magical ship that could destroy that entire vessel if the thing's turned on the wrong way." She dinged the mallet against the side of the bowl for emphasis.

"Well, you can't beat magic into submission." Nickie nudged her sister's arm with a loose fist. "Hey."

"What?" Emily tipped her head back to meet her big sister's gaze.

"We're gonna find her, okay? Whatever it takes. I'm not worried about that part."

With a sigh, Emily gazed at the singing bowl again and pressed her lips together. "You can hold off on telling me what part you're worried about."

"Did you have to cast any spells to get this thing working the last time?" Nathan asked.

"Nope. But we can try it this time." With the mallet in one hand, Emily stuck her other palm out over the center console and wiggled her fingers. "I need a magical jumpstart."

With a wry chuckle, Nickie grabbed her sister's hand.

The minute Emily drew the mallet along the bowl's rim,

both witches' rings flashed bright yellow. A bolt of red burst from the top of the singing bowl, then darted through the windshield and down Pressler Street. The bowl flew off Emily's lap, bounced off the dashboard, and landed on her foot. "Ow!" Quickly, she snatched up the bowl in both hands and brought it back up to safety.

"You okay?" Nickie asked as she shifted into drive.

"Way heavier things have crushed my toes." Emily buckled her seatbelt and tightened her grip on the mallet, ready to use it again when they needed another check-in with the magical tracker.

"Good." Nickie all but floored it, and they took off after the streak of light. "Despite how much that thing makes my head hurt, Em, it might be a good idea to keep using that mallet. I wanna make sure we don't miss a turn or anything."

Poising the mallet over the rim of the bowl, Emily couldn't hold back a triumphant smile. "You're giving me permission to make a sound that drives you nuts? Nonstop?"

"Don't push it."

Nickie took a sharp turn onto West 6th, and the singing bowl's low tones filled her car.

CHAPTER THREE

The singing bowl led them through Austin, throwing up red sparks whenever it felt like it. Emily kept the mallet moving around the rim, occasionally reaching out for Nickie's hand and the extra boost of magic brought by the Hadstrom sisters' contact.

When they got to Red River Street, the tracker's red bursts of light switched to orange, then bright yellow.

Emily squinted through her window, looking for magical explosions or unhinged Peabrain spells firing off without warning. A week ago, that would've been a sure sign of the gorafrex inside its human host. Now, though, magic was a headache for everyone. "Feels like we were just here."

"Because we were." Nickie pointed through her sister's window. "Brightwing Emporium."

"Oh, yeah. The fairy's apothecary. Hey, look, his lights are on. Think he's seen anything—" The singing bowl in Emily's lap shot off yellow and white sparks.

"Is it supposed to do that?" Nathan asked from the back seat, leaning forward.

"I don't know."

"What's going on, Em?"

"Wait." Emily fluttered her hand toward her sister. "Pull over."

"Why's it doing that?"

Nickie slowed and moved to the curb. Emily was no longer making the singing bowl sing, but the magical tracking device apparently had other plans. With a sigh, Nickie drummed her fingers on the steering wheel and watched the sparks. "Please tell me it's not broken too."

"Hey, if it is, it wasn't me." Emily spread her arms and stared at the bowl of fireworks in her lap. "White and yellow. That means we're close, right?"

"It's supposed to." Nickie leaned away from her sister and the exploding bowl. "But they're not giving us a direction."

"Still, that helps us narrow it down to—oh. Nope." Emily knocked the mallet against the side of the bowl a few times. "Come on."

Now the bowl spat orange and red sparks too, all four colors flying in every direction. Some of them whizzed through the back of the car past Nathan's head and disappeared behind them. The orange sparks shot straight up through the car's roof, and Emily craned her neck as if she could see past a few feet above her. "Well, I *know* Laura's not in the sky."

"So, this obviously isn't the normal MO for that thing," Nathan added.

"Ya think?" Nickie glanced at the rearview mirror and

caught the professor's gaze. When he shrugged, she added, "Sorry."

"Don't be. This is frustrating."

"Hold on, guys." Emily stared at the sparking bowl, which was starting to calm down and only spat a few bright motes instead of an explosion. "I can get this thing to work. Maybe it just needs another boost."

"Or maybe we need one of your potions to get it back on track."

Emily wrinkled her nose. "I can use a potion to do the same thing as a spell. Hopefully. But as far as I know, nothing I mix up's gonna *make* magic do its job again. Not sure how that works with tracking artifacts."

Nathan cleared his throat and tried not to stare too hard at the group of college-aged kids dressed up as superheroes walking down the sidewalk on Red River. "The potions might not be a bad idea."

"Yeah, I know they're not a bad idea. But we're already here." Emily took a deep breath, closed her eyes, and nodded. "I can do this. I can get it to work."

Nickie watched her sister for a few seconds, then held out her hand again. "Do what you gotta do, Em. We'll try one more time, but I think I'm with Nathan. Even Hadstrom-sister jumper cables don't look like they're working the way we want them to."

"Fine. One more shot." Emily grabbed her sister's hand, gritted her teeth at the singing bowl, and gently moved the mallet around the edge. The copper ring on her thumb flashed a muted light, and a thick column of red poured from the singing bowl before blasting down Red River in the direction they'd been moving.

A round of drunken cheers rose from the superheroes on the sidewalk. Nathan shook his head. "Normally, I *would* say it's not a good idea to keep that super-pumped tracker on like this, where everyone can see."

"It's working, isn't it?" Emily grinned. "Onward. Follow that light!"

Nickie shot her a confused look. "Let's keep the commands of excitement down, huh?"

"Right."

The car moved back out onto the street and followed the beacon of red light. They hadn't gone more than a block before the column sputtered out. "On it." Emily made the Tibetan bowl sing, and another flash burst from the bowl.

"Looks like we patched together a decent tracker." Nickie let herself hope that they were on the right path. *We're coming, Laura. Just hang in there a little.*

The tracker on their sister led them to Bogey Creek on the east side of Austin. The streaks of light had flared through red, orange, yellow, and finally white. Once Nickie parked and turned off the engine, the white lights darted every few seconds past the parking lot and into the trees. She grabbed the rolled-up apron full of clinking vials and stuck it under her arm. "Time to get out and follow, right?"

"Guess so." Emily opened her door to get out, cradling the singing bowl in her arms.

Nathan closed the back door behind him and looked at

the night sky. "It's not weird at all that the gorafrex took her out here into the park?"

"Not really." Emily shrugged and stepped over the low barricade at the edge of the parking lot. "We found an energy core in the habitat reserve the other day. In a giant pit."

"Really?"

"That's where we found Dave," Nickie added. "At this point, I'm not surprised by anything the gorafrex does. And with magic…"

"Right." Nathan followed the sisters down the path, the white bursts of light leading the way. "Everybody's just trying to make do with what they have. Which isn't much."

"We should be really close now." Emily looked up from the bowl every few seconds to follow the bursts of light, and the up-and-down head movement was starting to make her dizzy. "Really close."

"Stop." Nathan cocked his head, and the Hadstrom sisters shot him questioning glances. "You hear that?"

"No." Emily peered into the darkness of the tall oaks and dogwoods around them. "Should we be—"

Something rustled through the bushes on their right. Nickie stuck a hand into the folds of Emily's vial-filled apron. "Em," she whispered. "Which one is for explosions again?"

"Oh, great. *Now* you wanna go right for the explosives and—"

A huge boar barreled through the trees and darted across the path in front of them, squealing and grunting. It didn't pay any attention to the two witches and the part-Kashgar, part-Peabrain professor who'd stumbled onto the thing's nighttime run. Then it was gone, crashing through the trees. Only the hum of crickets and cicadas followed.

"Huh." Nathan scratched the back of his head and turned to look into the darkness the creature had darted out of. "You guys seen wild pigs like that running around before?"

"You mean, trailing pink streaks like that through the woods?"

"I meant just wild pigs." Nathan turned toward Emily and shrugged. "I thought the magic trail was a given."

"Nope. Never seen that before."

Nickie glanced at the bowl in her sister's arms. "We should focus on that thing. Any more tracking instructions?"

"Not so far."

The second Emily stepped forward along the path, the singing bowl exploded with light again in all the colors. Sparks and thick bursts shot through the trees around them, this time sounding very much like Emily had set fire to a box of fireworks just to see what would happen. The branches erupted, startled birds taking flight, squawking and shrieking.

"Well, it's impossible to follow now, isn't it?" Emily shouted over the ruckus.

"I don't think Laura's here," Nickie shouted back.

"Why not?" Nathan stepped closer, not wanting to add his voice to all the noise.

Nickie tapped her temple. "If Laura's with the gorafrex, that thing's drums would be pounding in my head by now."

When Emily said something else, both Nathan and Nickie shouted, "What?"

"I said, it makes sense! Take this." Emily shoved the mallet against Nathan's chest, which he took with wide eyes, and held the singing bowl's firework display out in front of her with both hands. "Now would be a great time to stop."

"This isn't normal, is it?" Nathan asked.

"Is anything?" Emily grinned at him, but her eyes were wild and more unsure than he'd seen them before. "This thing needs an off button." She shook the bowl, spilling light and spells out over the sides, and closed her eyes. Her copper legacy ring sputtered with dim light. "Cut it out!"

All the lights and the hissing and popping stopped immediately. The singing bowl bloomed from its copper color to deep crimson, then flared brighter into orange.

"Okay. See? That's much better. Now it's time to— Ow!" Emily dropped the bowl onto the dirt path and shook out her hands.

"Em…"

"Turned itself into a cauldron."

Nickie frowned at the bowl, which was covered in dirt. A few bits of Laura's graduation gown spilled out of the opening. "What?"

"It burned me, Nickie."

Nathan stooped and picked up the bowl, which was back to its normal copper color. "Seems fine to me."

"Great. So it's just me." Emily ran a hand over her hair. "Laura's not here, and our magical tracker doesn't work."

"Thinking about using potions now?" Nickie set a hand on her sister's shoulder and nodded.

"I really thought I could get this to work."

"I know, Em."

The forest settled down now that the singing bowl had stopped throwing its own party, and Nathan and the Hadstrom sisters turned back up the path to the parking lot. "I can do potions, no problem," Emily said, trudging behind her sister. "I was just trying to stick with what we know already works."

"We know the potions work," Nathan countered. "Everything else is pretty much a tossup at this point. It was a good try."

"It was a waste of time. I'm sorry."

"We don't have time for that, Em," Nickie said. "Just gotta keep moving forward."

Another grunting squeal rang out through the forest behind them. The trio spun around in time to see a bright pink light shoot straight up into the air. Then it moved through the trees, bouncing and wobbling behind the startled creature.

"What is up with that *pig*?"

CHAPTER FOUR

They pulled up in front of the Hadstrom sisters' house on Pressler Street. Nickie stared through the windshield for a few seconds, then unbuckled her seatbelt and pushed the driver's side door open. It was fast enough to show annoyance, and Emily sucked a sharp breath through her teeth.

"She okay?" Nathan asked from the back seat.

"I mean, as okay as anyone whose sister has been abducted to be the gorafrex's next blood-magic snack, right?" Immediately, she turned around to look at him. "Sorry. That was definitely too soon."

"Hey, I can take poorly timed jokes, no problem. I don't know what it's like to have a sibling *or* to have them taken, so maybe I don't want to get Laura back quite as much as you do. But I'm willing to bet it's close."

"Right." Emily turned around again and unbuckled her seatbelt. "I think you proved that much by not taking no for an answer. Nickie's fine. I'll just whip up some potions, and we'll get Laura, and then we'll work on putting magic back in its place. Boy, we've turned into the keepers of Austin's magical problems, huh?"

The only response she got was the back door opening as Nathan got out.

"And I'm talking too much." With a sigh, Emily opened her door and hefted the useless singing bowl under her arm again. Nickie was already at the top of the stairs heading toward the front door, Nathan close behind her. "Hey, anyone consider that thing might decide to turn around and come back for the rest of us?"

"Why would it do that?" Nathan asked.

"Well, I mean, it knows where we live. And we're the only magicals on this ship who can lock it up again. Or at least, two out of three." Emily ran jumped up the last step and jogged to catch up with the others.

"If it has a plan to come back for you or me, Em, I doubt the gorafrex would even try until it's gotten what it wants from Laura. Wouldn't be very smart to stick us all together in captivity and think we wouldn't be able to figure our own way out." Nickie stopped to readjust the apron. "But if all three of us have to be there to take it down, the gorafrex only needs one Hadstrom witch."

Emily stopped beside her sister and stared at the front of their house. "All good points, but that doesn't explain why our front door's open."

Nickie jerked her head up toward the porch. "You didn't close the door?"

"Of course, I closed the door. Right after Mr. I-Won't-Stay-Behind booked it for your car." Shooting a quick frown at her older sister, Emily readjusted the singing bowl until she gripped the rim tightly with both hands. "And it's not the kind of door that blows open with a draft."

"We got rid of the drafts."

"Yeah, I know."

"I'll go check it out," Nathan muttered, stepping past them. "Stay here."

"Yeah, right."

"Nice try."

The Hadstrom sisters overtook the physics professor on their way to the door. Nathan clenched his jaw and whispered, "Hey, if somebody's in there looking for the two of you, I can at least figure out who they are and what they want first. They're less likely to attack *me*. Probably."

"Really?" Nickie leaned toward him with wide eyes. "I'm pretty sure the gorafrex is the only magical busting into other people's homes and attacking them." She blinked and shrugged. "At least in Austin."

"But somebody broke in. If it makes you feel better, go ahead and count to five. Then you guys can come in after me." Nathan nodded, raised his hands, and gestured for them to wait as he stepped toward the cracked-open front door. "And I'm a pretty good negotiator."

"Fine," Nickie whispered.

Emily held up five fingers and nodded toward the door.

The Kashgar part of Nathan—which ran a lot less through his veins than his human Peabrain ancestry—gave him an eerie ability to walk without making a sound. Emily gripped the singing bowl even tighter when he moved over the few wooden slats that made a muffled, earthy crunch every time she stepped on them, but there was nothing. He nudged the door open another inch and slipped inside, and the Hadstrom sisters started counting.

"Who are you?" a man shouted.

Nickie and Emily exchanged glances. They knew that voice, and it wasn't Nathan's.

"I could ask you the same thing—"

The sisters darted for the open door, but someone inside their house closed it quickly. Emily slammed against the door and reeled back, dropping the singing bowl with a loud clang to grip her nose with both hands.

"You don't get to come in here and start asking *us* questions, whoever you are."

"I can explain if you give me just a minute," Nathan said.

"What would *you* know about my—stop!"

A burst of purple light lit up the dining room windows and spilled into the front yard. Emily dropped to pick up the bowl again, and Nickie twisted the doorknob with a jerk before shoving open the door. "Dad, stop!"

Emily darted inside behind her sister, her head tilted back as she pinched her bleeding nose. She turned sideways to eye Greg Hadstrom standing in the dining room, then her eyes widened. "*Mom?*"

"Careful." The Hadstrom sisters' dad pointed his wand at the other end of the foyer, where Nathan had fallen haphazardly against the bottom of the stairs and the wall into the living room. "Please tell me Kashgars breaking into your house isn't a regular thing."

"No, it's not." Nickie shot her dad a scathing glance and went to help Nathan up off the floor. The physics professor shook his head and tried to get his bearings. He slapped a hand against the wall to steady himself, and Nickie released him to turn toward her parents. "If anyone broke into our house, it'd be you two. What are you doing here?"

"Mom, I'm fine." Emily lifted the singing bowl in one hand to ward her mother off before Nancy Milton had a chance to look at her youngest's bloody nose. "I got it."

"Just let me see—"

"Nope." Emily walked past her parents into the dining room table, set down the bowl, and went to the bathroom behind the mudroom under the stairs for some tissues. "I can still hear you. Keep talking."

"We didn't break into your house, kiddo." Greg held up a spare key in one hand, his wand still trained on Nathan with the other. "But I would *really* like to know why a Kashgar just walked inside like he owns the place."

"Part-Kashgar," Nathan muttered, rubbing the sore spot on the back of his head. "I understand where the confusion comes from, though. Most people can't tell."

"That didn't answer my question."

"Greg."

"What?" The man turned around to raise his eyebrows at his ex-wife.

Nancy nodded toward his outstretched hand. "Put your wand away."

Only then did Greg Hadstrom realize that he still had his wand—which dealt almost exclusively in volatile magic these days—trained on Nathan's chest. He cleared his throat, lowered his wand halfway, and turned back to Nathan and Nickie. "Somebody better start talking."

A frustrated grunt came from the kitchen as Emily walked through it into the dining room, her nose plugged with twisted bits of toilet paper. "When I said keep talking, I meant you guys. As in, talk about why *both* of you are here at the same time at…" She jerked her phone out of her back pocket. "One o'clock in the morning."

"Where's Laura?" their mom asked.

Emily blinked, then clenched her eyes shut and sighed. "Forgot to update you on that one, didn't we?"

"Your mom told me what happened," Greg added. "Or at least the part about the two of you rushing out of her house to get back home. And Laura's not answering her phone."

"That's 'cause she doesn't have it." Nickie gestured toward the living room, where her big sister's cell phone sat on the coffee table. "It took her, Dad."

"*What?*"

"Yeah. Showed up before we did." Emily prodded her nose swollen with toilet paper. "We saw it just before it popped out *with* Laura. Pretty much where you're standing, actually. Tried to stop it."

When she pointed at the far wall of the dining room, both their parents turned around to see the charred crater Emily's last-ditch spell had left there a few hours before. "Well," Greg took a deep breath, "I guess that explains why it looks like a wrecking crew moved through the place."

"That wasn't us," Nickie said.

"Oh, yeah. Speaking of." Emily pointed at her parents, her finger wagging from one to the other. "How come you guys didn't tell us Speed's a were-bulldog fighting machine? That would've been a nice piece of information to know *before* we barged in on him fighting the gorafrex like his life depended on it."

"Probably did."

"Greg." Nancy shot her ex a worried frown and nodded at their daughters. "The most important thing is that Laura's been taken, and we need to get her back."

"Of course, that's the most important part, Nance. I'd never argue with you on that. If I was the kind of person who liked to argue about things." Greg paused, shook his head, and glanced around his daughters' destroyed house. "Speed's a guardian, girls. Has been in our family for, I mean, as long as he's been alive. Which is...what?"

"Since my ancestors stepped foot on this ship for its first voyage," Nancy added. "Or what was *supposed* to be the first."

"Okay. We have a legacy to guard a witch-killer who got out by mistake *and* the ultimate fighting machine stuffed into a tiny, lazy, farting, immortal bulldog package." Emily spread her arms and stared at her parents. This time, though, her usual joking grin was gone. "Thanks for passing down the most ridiculous combination of family heirlooms, guys."

"Speed protected my mother," Nancy said. "Which I knew about only because she told me the stories. I didn't need him for anything, but it looks like he showed up when he was required."

"We got here too late." Nickie turned toward the living room. "We have a place to sit, guys. Let's—oh. No, we don't." Taking in the broken armchair, the rug smooshed up against the wall, and the toppled couch in the living room, Nickie sighed. "Dining room table, then?"

CHAPTER FIVE

Greg and Nancy exchanged glances, then turned silently and pulled chairs out from beneath the table. Nickie, Emily, and a sore Nathan followed. All three of them sat across the table from the Hadstrom sisters' parents. "Mom, I'm sorry we didn't tell you what happened right away."

"You have a lot going on. I get that." Nancy sat back in her chair and folded her hands in her lap. "But I called you both, and nobody picked up."

"You called us?" Emily pulled the toilet paper from her nose and sniffed. "Oh. We were at Bogey Creek."

"Did you find her?" Greg asked.

"Nope. This stupid bowl worked really well all two times we had to use it. And then it just..." Emily mimed an explosion, complete with sound effects.

"I don't think I've seen one of those before," Greg said.

"It tracks magical frequencies," Nickie said. "Laura bought it from Hopkins Antiques—"

"Oh!" Emily jumped up from her chair and headed back toward the foyer. "Potions. I gotta…"

Nickie stared after her sister until the house filled with a rumbling groan. A wall slid into place where the entrance to the foyer had been, and the rest of the house shifted around Emily to take her to whatever room she wanted.

"You told us about that part," Nancy muttered, her head cocked as she listened to the house shifting around her youngest daughter. "But I don't think I've been here to see it yet."

"Yeah, it's pretty cool." Nickie stood from the table and pressed her palms against its surface. "We can talk about the cool stuff later. As soon as she comes back, we're going out to look for Laura again."

Nancy glanced from Nathan to Nickie and offered a weak smile. "Don't you think you should—"

"I'll come with you." Greg stood abruptly from the table and swished his wand eagerly. Purple light burst from the tip and added another, albeit smaller, charred crater in the dining room wall. He stared at the destruction, then wiggled his jaw in agitation. "I just can't get used to this. The most practiced wizards in this town are blowing their kids' houses up."

"Greg, please." Nancy nodded at his wand, and her ex sniffed.

"Yeah." He stuck his wand in his back pocket and dusted off his hands. Then he met Nickie's gaze and rubbed his chin. "Listen, kiddo. I know I'm not much help where the gorafrex is concerned. That ring wouldn't work for me if I wore it again."

"Doesn't work for me, either." Nickie glanced at the

black legacy ring Greg had worn when the responsibility was with him and his siblings. "At this point, I'm willing to try anything."

When she started to twist off the ring, Greg waved her off. "No, no. I know you're talking about magic being...well, less predictable than your Aunt Julie, am I right?" He glanced at Nancy, who just closed her eyes and let out a slow breath. "Or not. But the ring's yours, Nickie. My time's over, and it only responds to you."

"Barely."

"*But* I might be able to help you find Laura if you and Emily will— I'm sorry." Greg turned his attention to Nathan, still sitting in his seat, and cocked his head. "How do you know my daughters?"

Nathan sat up a little straighter in his chair. "Laura and I share a hall between our offices."

"Seriously?" Nickie stared down at him and folded her arms.

"It's true," Nathan said. "Maybe now's not the—"

"This is Nathan." Nickie gestured toward him and stared at her dad. "Part-Kashgar, mostly Peabrain, physics professor at UT, and Laura's boyfriend."

Nathan pressed his lips together and slowly turned his head to look at Greg and Nancy again. "Nice to meet you both."

"Boyfriend." Greg blinked. "Huh."

"Stop." Nancy slapped his wrist with the back of her hand and smiled at Nathan. "I'm Nancy. This is Greg. Nice to meet you too, Nathan."

"Boyfriend."

"She's not sixteen, Greg."

"I *know* that. I just…" The man scratched his head and finally shrugged. Despite his shock, Greg leaned over the table and extended a hand. "Yeah, good to meet you. Probably would've been better under different circumstances."

"That's why I didn't say anything." Nathan stood and shook Greg's hand, then rubbed his hands together and glanced at the wall blocking them from the foyer and the front door. "I'm here to help for as long as takes to find Laura."

"And you know about everything they're involved in?" Nancy asked.

"Yep. Laura asked me for help with some runes a little over a week ago, so she had to tell me. I know it's on the three of them to put that thing back in its prison, but I can't just wait to hear what happened next. Not now."

"Good man." Greg pointed at the professor, then jerked his finger away and stared at it as if the broken magic coursing through Austin might shoot out of his fingertips at any minute. Then he reached back and patted his wand in his back pocket. "What's Emily doing again?"

"Potions, Dad." Nickie turned toward the foyer, but the wall was still there.

"When did that start?"

"Just a few days ago. She's really into it."

Nancy stood from the table too. "That's my girl. I'm glad she's picking up some of her heritage. It's great to carve a new path, but there's nothing like using what your family gave you."

"I know." Nickie wrinkled her nose at her mom. "Maybe let her think it's *her* thing for a little longer and not something you gave her, okay?"

Nancy narrowed her eyes at her middle daughter. "Why?"

"She's been having trouble with figuring out what she wants. With magic. And life, maybe. I'm not gonna get into it with you guys right now, and you should probably ask her. Later."

"If she needs help, though, I'm always here."

"Yeah, we know, Mom."

"They'll figure it out," Greg said.

Nancy turned to look at him and let out a wry laugh. "You just said you wanted to go with them to help."

"I didn't say I wanted to go *with* them." Greg huffed and tried to hide it behind a smile. "I said I wanted to help."

"Of course, we do." Nancy turned back toward Nickie and nodded. "Is there any way we can help?"

"Unless you have a magically foolproof way of finding Laura, *without* her cell phone, 'cause that's here…"

The house rumbled again, groaning and shifting as walls folded and slid around. The wall blocking them from the foyer sank down into the floor, and Emily walked quickly into the dining room with a red plastic bucket of all the supplies she'd gathered from wherever she'd gone. Glass clinked when she set the bucket on the table.

"So, I know we don't—" The youngest Hadstrom sister looked at her parents and froze. "You're still here."

"Yes, Emily." Nancy nodded. "Did you just pile everything for potions together into a plastic bucket?"

"It's exactly what it looks like." Emily turned her attention to taking out vial after jar after tin box from the bucket and spreading them out on the table. "Nickie, can you grab some—"

"Yep." Nickie shot her parents a warning look and headed into the kitchen for mixing bowls and whatever seemed remotely appropriate for making potions.

"So you're really into this stuff, huh?" Greg asked, leaning over the table to watch his daughter work.

"Yeah. Really into it. Pretty good at it. Kinda hating myself right now that we wasted so much time with that stupid bowl."

"And you've used these before?"

"Yes, Dad. I've made potions before, and I've used them before, and they work just the way I want them to every time." She paused to look up at her parents. "It's the only thing we can rely on right now because magic blew a fuse after the gorafrex powered two energy cores in a— You know what? I'd love to tell you all about it. *After* we find Laura, and *after* that thing's behind iron again. I gotta—" She returned to the vials and jars to organize them.

"I recognize that bucket," Nancy said.

"Got it from the greenhouse."

"That's right. A garden and a potions lab go hand in hand. Grow your own ingredients, right? How's it lookin' in there?"

"Not good." Emily whipped out her phone and scrolled through her photos to find the ingredients from the books in the main library's magical restricted section. "It's a flesh-eating jungle right now, but we have bigger problems."

"A flesh-eating what?" Greg chuckled and pulled his shirt collar away from his neck. Emily was absorbed in skimming through the recipe on her phone and separating her ingredients, so her dad turned to Nathan. "You know anything about the greenhouse problem?"

Nathan glanced at Emily. "Not really."

"Okay, here." Nickie stepped back into the dining room with an armful of bowls and measuring spoons and a whisk. "Anything else?"

Emily glanced up for a second. "Nope. That's good. Oh! We still have some of those Sterno cans, right?"

"Uh, yeah."

"Nickie, wait," Nancy said, holding up a finger for her middle child to stop. "I don't think mixing any of these ingredients over an open flame is a good ide—"

"Mom, I know what I'm doing." Emily didn't look up from the potions.

"I know you do, Emily. But I really think you should—"

"When I want your advice, I'll ask for it, okay?" Emily opened her hand toward her sister. "Tablespoon."

"Yep." Nickie dropped it into her sister's hand, then turned back toward the kitchen.

"Oh, grab one of those shakers too."

"*Shakers?*" Nancy stared at her ex, and Greg shrugged. "Does it call for a shaker in that recipe?"

"Mom. Please."

"Okay." Her mother lifted both hands and stepped back, but she watched Emily work with a concerned frown. Her wand slipped into her fingers, and she held it at the ready, just in case.

"Anything I can do?" Nathan asked.

"Yeah. Stand there and entertain my parents for a few minutes." When the youngest Hadstrom sister looked up at Greg and Nancy, she snorted, then wiggled her eyebrows at him. "Kidding."

"Sterno and fire." Nickie lit the Sterno and set it carefully down away from the potions ingredients.

"Emily?"

"Thanks, Mom. I got it."

"Nickie? A little help?"

Nickie stepped back at shook her head at their mother. "It's *her* thing."

Nathan took a slow, careful step away from the table.

"Right, but there's still— No, no. Don't mix those two toge—"

Emily set down the jars she'd just opened and took a deep breath. "Okay, I made two different potions last night that would make you run screaming if I told you what they were, but they're perfect. So please just let me do this."

"You know how volatile those two are when you mix them—"

"Mom!" Emily slammed her hands on the table, and her copper legacy ring flashed. All the chairs around the dining room table toppled over, followed by the singing bowl and the ring of measuring spoons, which flew into the kitchen and hit the cabinets with a metallic jingle.

The dining room fell perfectly still.

Greg licked his lips and stared at his daughter's copper ring. "I haven't seen that before."

"A lot of things are happening that no one's seen before," Nickie stated.

"True."

Emily got her breathing back under control and looked at her parents. "The only thing that works is potions. I know what I'm doing, and it's really hard to concentrate on what I need with both of you hovering over me like I'm— Mom. Why do you have your wand out?"

Nancy's eyes widened, and she tried to maintain her collected appearance by eying the thin branch powering her magic. "You told your sister to light a Sterno."

For a second, Emily was on the verge of another outburst, but then she broke into a grin. "You have no idea how long I've wanted to say this."

Her mom looked stunned. "What?"

"Put your wand away, Mom."

Greg barked a laugh and immediately covered up with a fit of coughing. Nancy's lips twitched at the corners, and she clearly stifled a laugh as she pocketed her wand and stepped toward her youngest daughter.

"Okay." Nancy placed a quick kiss on Emily's temple, then lifted her hands. "You do what you need to do to get the job done. We know you will."

"Of course, we do," Greg added. "Never a doubt in our minds."

"Great." Emily nodded at her parents, then got back to work.

Nickie walked her parents into the foyer toward the front door. "Go home. Chill out. Get some sleep. We've got it covered."

"If I didn't know better, I'd say this is what being parented by your kids looks like."

Nancy shot her husband a knowing glance. "That's exactly what it is."

"And it's what we all need right now." Nickie hugged her parents goodbye, then opened the door. "We'll call you when we know anything else, okay? Promise."

Nancy smoothed her hair away from her daughter's forehead and nodded. "Good. And be careful with the Sterno, huh?"

Nickie closed her eyes and nodded.

"That's our cue to go." Nudging Greg's shoulder, Nancy stepped outside.

"Right behind you." Greg paused and leaned toward Nickie. "How are *you* doin'?"

"Fine, all things considered. My playing's a little different recently, but that's music as magic for ya, right?"

"Among other things." He gave her a sympathetic smile and kissed the top of her head. "Hang in there. Laura's resourceful enough to have a few tricks up her sleeve. You and Emily have the time to do this right, okay?"

"I know. We just don't know how much time."

"Well, I'm willing to bet that if the rest of us are having this kinda trouble with magic right now, so is the gorafrex. That buys us all some time. And I didn't want to interrupt your sister's flow with her mad-witch science experiments, but…"

Nickie snorted as her dad turned to glance at Emily, who was hard at work while Nathan watched in silence.

"You guys should check the library again."

"Magical restricted?"

"Yeah. Your mom's speech about 'using what's handed down to you' sparked a memory. I found something in one of the books there a long time ago. Lost interest, and I can't remember the name of the book. It didn't seem nearly as important to me then as it does now." Greg rubbed his chin again and nodded. "Some of those books have notes in the margins, right? Friendly tips. That kinda thing. I only found one, but it was written for our family. *By* our family. There may be more, but it's worth a shot. Depending on how much whoever wrote them knew about our family's job here on this ship."

"Wow. So Hadstrom wizards and witches have been defacing super-old magical books from the Library of Alexandria for generations, huh?"

Greg laughed and grabbed her shoulder. "Just in case someone else needed to see it."

"Thanks, Dad." As she watched him step through the front door and head toward Nancy standing on the sidewalk, Nickie frowned. "Did you guys *walk* here from Mom's?"

"Nope." Greg gestured up Pressler Street. "Parked a few houses down in case someone did break into your house. They'd never see us coming." The man squinted and pulled a sloppy martial-arts pose.

Nickie tried to laugh but couldn't quite make it sound believable. "Okay. Be safe."

"'Night, kiddo. Don't forget to sleep." He pointed at her, then turned around and rubbed his neck as he caught up with his ex.

Closing the door, Nickie blinked, then headed back into the dining room. "Our parents are paranoid."

"Oh, yeah?" Emily wasn't paying attention.

"They parked up the street so the *criminals who broke into our house* wouldn't see them coming."

"Sneaky." Emily finished her carefully measured pour of glowing green sludge into one of the mixing bowls.

"I almost wonder how often they park up the street to watch us when things are *normal*."

With a snorted laugh, Emily stirred her newest potion and tipped her head back and forth. "They have lives too. And not nearly enough time to stand out behind the bushes waiting for their kids to do something weird."

"I mean, they wouldn't have to stand there very long."

Both Hadstrom sisters laughed, but it died quickly under the pressure of what Emily was trying to do. She picked up another bottle, unscrewed the lid with a dropper attached, and let a single drop of black liquid fall into the bowl. The green-sludge mixture bubbled and let out a stream of smoke, then turned orange. With the second drop, the potion was clear again.

"Okay." Emily nodded at the flame in the Sterno. "Time to play with fire."

CHAPTER SIX

Emily set the Pyrex dish on top of one of the racks they'd taken from the oven. The rack wobbled a little on the stacked boxes they'd put under it to keep it high enough over the Sterno's flame, but then it settled.

"There." Stripping off her matching oven mitts, she tapped her phone's screen to look for the next part of the recipe. "Shouldn't take too long. I think."

"So, I just have to ask." Nathan leaned away from the table. "And please don't take this as anything other than pure curiosity. Was your mom right about the no-fire rule?"

"Oh, totally."

"Emily…"

"It's okay." Emily patted her sister's shoulder. "I'm not worried. The recipe calls for some kind of warming spell. Obviously, I'm not gonna try to heat this stuff with my magic, so we're going old-school."

"With fire. If that gets too hot—"

"Yeah!" Emily scrambled to put her gloves back on, then

watched the dish of clear liquid. A small neon-orange spark flared in the center, and she quickly lifted the dish off the rack. "But it didn't. Look at that."

Nickie watched her sister set the ridiculously dangerous potion down on a baking sheet on the table and bit her lip. "I hope you're totally sure about that."

"Mostly sure, yeah." Emily walked around the table and picked the singing bowl up off the floor. She pulled a face and reached gingerly into it before jerking out Laura's graduation cap and gown. The cap thumped onto the table, and she took the gown with her to her workplace at the head of the table. "So here we go."

"You're gonna use her graduation stuff again?"

"We didn't find anything much better, did we?" Emily twisted a sleeve of the gown into a tight wad. "It's not like this lost its meaning for her when the singing bowl screwed up."

Nickie shrugged and folded her arms. "Fine by me. I'm just lookin' out for you, you know? In case that potion leaves some kinda mark on Laura's *symbolic garment*."

With a sharp laugh, Emily lifted the gown's rolled sleeve toward the finished potion in the dish. "Guess we'll just have to see what happens."

She dipped the sleeve into the bowl and sloshed it around, then pulled it back out and let most of the liquid drip into the dish.

Nathan leaned forward for a closer look. "Is it supposed to do something, or..."

"Not sure." Emily set the potion-soaked sleeve on the baking sheet and studied her phone. "Crap!"

"Em?"

With a heavy sigh, the youngest Hadstrom sister bowed her head and leaned over the head of the table, propping herself up with her hands. "I get too excited. I know that. I need to stop and go all the way through."

"What'd you miss?" Nickie joined her sister to look at the recipe in the photo. "Oh."

"So?" Nathan stared at them and waited.

"My sister missed the part about an eight-hour settling period." Nickie patted Emily's back and turned away from the table. "That's how long we have to wait for something to happen."

"Eight hours." Gazing at the ceiling, Nathan shoved his hands into his pockets and forced himself to breathe slowly. "This is the only tracking spell you have?"

"Yeah." Emily straightened and drummed her fingers on the table. "I didn't have much time to spend at the library, 'cause I had to go into work. And I only got through one book. I'm sure there are others, but I don't have the recipes."

"Right. Well, there's a silver lining. Probably."

Emily finally looked up at him and widened her eyes. "So let's hear it, Nate. I could use one of those right now."

He gestured toward the soaked gown and the dish on the oven rack. "It gives us an excuse to try getting some sleep. Maybe even a full eight hours."

"Yeah, that's realistic," Emily muttered.

"Or however much we can. Seriously. It's getting late. Last time I was up this late, Laura and I fell asleep at the..." Nathan cleared his throat, and his mouth twitched into a smile that was more worried than reassuring. "I don't do very well on less than seven hours."

"Part of being in your thirties, huh?" Nickie asked with a smirk.

He let out a dry chuckle. "Something like that. And in the morning, if this potion doesn't show us what we want to know, the library will be open."

"The library." The defeat drained from Emily's face, and she nodded. "Yeah. More potions, more answers. If I can even get in."

"It's worth a shot." Nathan headed past the Hadstrom sisters toward the front door. "I'll be back around nine. We can go from there."

"Sure." Nickie stepped into the foyer with him. "You can stay here if you want. All we gotta do is turn the couch back over the right way. Instant bed."

"I appreciate that. But unless you guys have a change of clothes for somebody who's six-five and an extra toothbrush lying around, I gotta go home anyway." Nathan gave her a tired smile and opened the front door. "My phone's on if anything happens. Or I'll just be back at nine."

"Okay. Drive safe."

"Yep." The professor slipped out the front door and shut it behind him.

Nickie let out a long breath. "All right. I agree with him about the sleep part, Em."

"Yeah, I know." Emily turned around and shook her head. "I'm messing up tonight."

"Come on." Guiding her sister toward the staircase, Nickie almost had to push Emily up the stairs to the second floor. "You're doing everything you know how to do right now. Which, honestly, is a lot more than the zero ideas my brain's been throwing out. Your potions work. No matter how much Mom freaks out about it."

Emily snorted and finally stopped dragging her feet. "Did you see her face when I told her to put her wand away?"

"She looked like she was about to crack up harder than Dad. Did that just come to you in the moment?"

Emily shrugged. "I think I put it on my bucket list somewhere around fifth grade. Which, I'm pretty sure, was the year I got grounded the most. I mean, out of every other year."

"Long time comin', then." Nickie huffed out a laugh as they reached the second-floor landing and headed toward their rooms at the end of the hall. She ducked her head and whispered, "By the way, Dad gave me some helpful hints before he left. At least, I hope they're helpful."

"Was it a secret or something?" Emily stopped at her bedroom door and cocked her head. "I *can* keep a secret."

"He just didn't wanna bother you. You know, with all the flying things when you're frustrated."

"I'm working on it. What did he say?"

Nickie leaned against the doorway into her room. "That he thinks he remembers some kind of Hadstrom-family notes written in the restricted books at the main library."

Her sister's eyes widened. "*What?*"

"Back from when he still wore the ring and had no idea that the gorafrex was anything more than a legend and Hadstrom tradition." Nickie grinned. "But I figured that might cheer you up. As much as either of us can cheer up right now."

"Are you kidding me?" Emily grinned, wiggled her eyebrows, and opened her bedroom door. "This is like *The Half-Blood Prince* Hadstrom-style. Of course, I'm cheered up. I mean, not… I'm cheered up to the level of 'let's do this and get Laura back.'"

"I know, Em. We'll head down to the main library tomorrow. 'Night."

"'Night." The witches' bedroom doors closed within seconds of each other. Emily turned around and slumped back against hers with a heavy sigh. "I didn't think it was possible to be this worried about Laura *and* this excited about finding clues in highly restricted library books."

On her queen-sized bed, their immortal bulldog Speed lay sprawled on his back, all four paws dangling at various angles, his mouth hanging open. A long, grating snore escaped him, and his jowls puffed out with his breaths.

"And *you*." Emily grabbed her pajama shorts and tank top from their pile on the floor and changed into them. "You turned into a deadly Hadstrom guardian and fought the gorafrex *all by yourself*. Or I guess the gorafrex and its host's Peabrain magic. That's some serious stuff, buddy."

Speed didn't move, even when she climbed up onto the mattress with him. "And apparently you heal super-fast, too. Look at you." Emily ran a hand down the dog's belly, where the bruises that had swelled under his skin and the gashes that had been bleeding just a few hours ago were now almost completely gone—a greenish color under his tan fur and that was it. "You did your best too, didn't you? It was perfect. We wouldn't even know where she went or who had her right now if you hadn't been around."

With a sigh, Emily wiggled her way under the covers

and lay back on her pillow, staring at the ceiling. "I'm giving the weredog more credit than the witch who makes explosive potions in under half an hour. That's me, by the way." She glanced down at Speed, lying perfectly still beside her feet.

The dog snored again.

"I'll get this done. We'll figure it out." Emily closed her eyes and tried to relax. "Hang in there, Laura."

CHAPTER SEVEN

A constant muted knocking woke Emily up the next morning. When she realized it wasn't the thump of her chef's knife coming down over and over again into a potions vial shaped like a giant carrot, she groaned and slowly pushed herself up. "Weird dream. Makes sense, though, if I'm trading cooking for—"

She gasped and whipped the covers off before leaping to the floor. It took her a minute to fumble through her jeans until she remembered she hadn't brought her phone upstairs with her. "No. Crap."

Speed snorted and rolled over when Emily threw open her bedroom door and ran down the hall. Her feet pounded on the creaky steps she took two at a time. Bare feet squeaked against the hardwood floors, Emily rounded the corner into the dining room, and barely stopped herself from knocking into the head of the table. "Please, no."

When she snatched up her phone and stabbed at the screen to wake it up, all the nervous energy escaped her in a huge sigh. "That was *way* too close, Em. What were you thinking?" The time on her clock read 7:37 a.m., which wasn't anywhere near a full eight hours of sleep. But her shift today at Meadowlark started at 8:00 a.m.

Clutching a handful of her hair, Emily stared at her phone and headed into the kitchen. The coffeemaker called her name, but right now, coffee had to take a back seat. "Am I really gonna do this? I have to. I'm really gonna..." She groaned, pulled up the number, and hesitated for only a second before pressing the call button.

While the line rang, she went through a few rounds of dry-heave practice.

"Meadowlark Tavern."

"It's Hadstrom," Emily croaked.

"Woah."

"I'm on this morning, but I..." She threw a dry heave in there just for fun.

"Yeah, keep that crap at home and out of my kitchen." Chef Ansler sighed. "You picked a pretty bad time to call in."

"I've been up since five trying to shove this thing into a deep, dark—" *Heave.*

"Christ, Hadstrom. You're gonna make *me* sick. You have the schedule on you?"

"Yeah."

"Call around. Chenoyl is usually pretty good about picking up this early. Tell him I said to call him first."

Emily let another gurgle build in her throat, then sighed. "I'll get it covered. Sorry, Chef."

"Just get better. And when you do, you're gonna ask whoever wants a day off if you can work their shift. We'll move things around. I need you in my kitchen, Hadstrom. Got it?"

"Yes, Che—" Emily let out a particularly convincing groan.

"Go back to bed."

The youngest Hadstrom sister hadn't expected to feel this ecstatic about her boss at the five-star restaurant hanging up on her, but she grinned at the phone and set it on the small kitchen table. "He needs me in his kitchen."

With a barely subdued laugh, she headed for the coffeemaker on the counter and fixed a pot. By the time she pressed the On button, she wasn't nearly as pleased with herself. "What did I *do*?"

Emily dragged her hands down her face and leaned back against the counter. When she dropped them again and opened her eyes, Nickie was standing in the doorway into the kitchen, frowning at her. "What happened?"

"The first thing on my list of things that should never happen."

"Em, this isn't a good time to leave me hangin'."

"I…" Emily gritted her teeth and clenched her eyes shut, as if the awful flu she'd pretended to have was giving her physical pain. "I called in to work." Her hands came up over her face again with a muffled slap.

"You…" Nickie took a deep breath and tried to pick one of the dozen responses bursting through her mind at once. Finally, she settled on a short, loud laugh. "You did it."

"I *know*." With her face still in her hands, Emily bent over and slumped back against the counter. "I promised myself I'd never miss a day."

Nickie approached her sister, grabbed Emily's wrists,

and removed her hands from her face while hauling her sister all the way back up. "Okay, first of all, I'm pretty sure that when your sister gets kidnapped by an insanely powerful magical creature with no body of its own bent on sucking the life out of witches for blood magic, you get a pass from work. Second, I thought that something horrible had happened, and I almost lost it. So don't do that again."

Emily stared at her sister and didn't lower her hands when Nickie released her. "It *was* awful."

"Given the circumstances, Em."

The youngest Hadstrom sister's hands slapped down on her thighs, and she shrugged. "Fair enough."

"How'd he take it?"

"Chef Ansler?" Emily frowned at the linoleum floor between them and cocked her head. "I mean, he sounded pretty grossed out, but I laid it on pretty thick."

"Uh…"

"Oh. I told him I was sick. And I might have almost hurled a few times."

Nickie held back a laugh, a little of it still snorting out her nose, and pointed at her sister. "You called into work, pretending to be sick."

"Yeah. And he told me to get better, 'cause he *needs me in his kitchen.*" Emily pulled her lips back in an unsure grimace. "That's something I can be happy about right now?"

"Is that a question?"

"No?"

Nickie burst out laughing and tapped her sister's shoulder. Emily moved out of the way, and Nickie reached into the cabinet for two mugs as the coffeemaker hissed and burbled on the counter. "That's definitely good. He doesn't want you there, he *needs* you there."

"That's what he said."

"And you have a free pass today. You got your shift covered, and we can go down to the library and not have to worry about—"

"Oh!" Emily jumped toward the kitchen table and snatched up her phone again. "Thanks for reminding me."

"Of what?"

The youngest Hadstrom sister walked through the mudroom under the stairs and into the living room, scrolling through her phone.

Nickie watched her go and slowly set the mugs down on the counter. "Okay."

Thick nails clicked across the second floor and thumped with aching slowness down the stairs, and finally, Speed came waddling into the kitchen. His tongue lolled from the side of his mouth, and he walked right up to Nickie before sitting back on his haunches and staring at her.

"Hey, bud." She bent to scratch him behind the ears, then ran her hand down his back. "You're looking a lot better after last night. I mean, wow! Not a scratch. Wherever you came from, I'm glad you hopped on this ship when you did."

Speed grunted and pressed his wet nose against her hand, then waddled into the mudroom. It took him a few tries to get one hind leg over the lip of the dog door, then the flap clicked shut behind him. Nickie chuckled. A groan and a loud dry heave came from the living room, and she stepped into the mudroom to watch her sister's theatrics.

Emily leaned against the side of the overturned couch—they had to put the living room back together soon—and gasped for breath. "Thanks, Chenoyl. I owe you one. Yeah, yeah. I'll—" She heaved again, noticed Nickie watching her, and winked. "Sorry. You pick the date. No problem. Yeah, I will." When she ended the call, Emily wiggled her phone at her sister and joined Nickie in the kitchen again. "You think I should get into acting?"

"Ha. Don't quit your day job." Nickie poured them both a cup of coffee and returned the pot to let the rest of it finish brewing. "That did sound pretty real, though."

"I mastered that one in sixth grade."

"Seriously?"

"Remember Nurse Bowlin? I even got her to think *she* was gonna be sick a few times. Haven't used it since the time Mom called me out on it at Christmas the year after, but still. Just like riding a bike."

With nothing to say to that, Nickie handed her sister a steaming mug and brought her fresh coffee to her lips. Halfway through the first sip, she jerked forward and headed for the dining room.

"That looked real too." Emily followed her. "More like surprise, though. Or like you just remembered something super important. If you wanna fake being sick—oh."

Both sisters stared at the baking sheet on the dining room table, with the tracking potion still in the Pyrex dish and Laura's wadded graduation gown still saturated with it. "What time is it?" Nickie asked.

"Almost eight." Emily walked around the table and studied the potion. "Does it look any different to you?"

"Not really. Is it supposed to?"

"Recipe just said give it at least eight hours, so..."

"Okay. Then we wait. Unless you wanna head to the library now. It'll be open by the time we get there."

Emily nodded, bent even lower to squint first at the dish of potion and then at Laura's gown, and nodded. "Let's wait. If this works—and it *should*, because I did it perfectly—I wanna be here when that dumb dress shows us where to find our sister."

"Sounds good." Nickie brought her coffee up to her lips again for another sip.

The front door burst open, and she just managed to keep most of the coffee in the cup as she jerked it away from her. Hot coffee sloshed onto the floor and all over her legs. "Aw!"

CHAPTER EIGHT

"Nickie?" Chuck stormed down the foyer and glanced into the living room, then turned and saw two Hadstrom sisters staring at him with coffee cups poised right over the table. "Oh, man. Hi."

"Hey, babe." Nickie glanced at her sister and tried not to let her eyes grow any wider than they already were. She set the dripping mug on the table just before Chuck wrapped her in a crushing hug. "Woah, hi. Is everything okay?"

Her boyfriend-turned-manager released her, grabbed her face with both hands, and kissed her fiercely before leaning back again. "Well, *now*, yeah. Why didn't you call me?"

"I mean, I just woke up—"

"You guys got some sleep, then. Good. Okay." Chuck took a deep breath and nodded over Nickie's shoulder. "Hey, Em."

"Hi."

"You figure out where she is?"

"Woah, woah. Slow down a sec." Nickie grabbed her

boyfriend's shoulders and tried to look reassuring and serious. "Are you okay?"

"Me? Yeah. Not the most important thing right now, though, is it?"

"So, you know about Laura." Emily sipped her coffee.

"Yeah." Chuck stuck his hands in his back pockets and nodded, taking in what looked like a middle school science experience on the dining room table. "I texted Nathan this morning."

"About what?" Nickie had a hard time picturing that conversation, especially this early in the morning, but she was willing to hear the explanation.

"What?" Chuck stared back and forth between the Hadstrom sisters. "He's a cool dude. We were talking about doing this— You know what? That doesn't matter. Point is, he told me about Laura. Said you guys were fine. But I had to…"

Nickie rubbed his arm and nodded. "We're fine. Nobody's coming to kidnap *us*."

"Yet," Emily added.

Chuck shot her a look and swallowed. "Well, I didn't know. And calling you doesn't work half the time anymore. More than half the time. So I got over here as fast as I could."

"Yeah, I can see that." Nickie stepped back to take in the man's gym shorts, mismatched flipflops, and the fact that his t-shirt was on backwards. "I'm so sorry I didn't let you know last night."

"We kinda forgot to tell everybody else, actually." Emily leaned against the table, eyeing the unchanged potion, and sipped more coffee.

"How did Nathan find out?"

"He called Laura's phone, which she left here. And then he came over, and we went looking for her, but…well, nothing so far."

"Okay. You'll figure it out." Chuck wrapped his arm around Nickie and pulled her against him, then studied the table again. "What's all this?"

"Tracking spell." Emily wrinkled her nose. "One that's taking its own sweet time."

"Don't you guys have a bowl for that or something?"

Nickie laughed. "Yep. Remember the whole 'magic's broken because a few energy cores have been turned on by blood magic' thing?"

"Oh." Chuck scratched his head with one hand and pulled her closer with the other. "I'm tryin', babe, but I feel like it's hard to keep up with what's going on."

"You and all of Austin, Chuck," Emily muttered, still staring at the potion. "Don't beat yourself up about it."

"You, uh, you guys seem a little…" Chuck cleared his throat. "Calm right now."

"No point in freaking out," Emily said. "Gotta take our time and do this right, you know? And if this doesn't work, which it definitely will, we still have a backup plan."

"Oh, yeah?"

Nickie wrapped her arm around his waist and looked up at him with what she thought was a hopeful smile. "Dad said our family's been secretly stashing hidden messages for future Hadstroms in some library books."

"You mean, like, for just anyone to pick up and find? That kinda goes against the whole 'Peabrains forgot their magic, so don't tell them' part." Chuck's mouth quirked sideways in confusion.

"Chuck." Emily finally pulled her gaze away from her potion to look at him. "There's a magical wall in the back of the main library that's basically made of security wards. Magicals go in and out, unawakened Peabrains only *stay* out, and the hidden room is full of magical books. Most of them saved from the Library of Alexandria before it burned down. Not even remotely close to how much *that* library had, but it's enough to keep the knowledge alive on this ship, as it were."

Blinking slowly, Chuck dipped his head and tried to process the info dump. "Okay. Sounds cool."

"It is." Nickie gave him a little squeeze. "I can show you sometime if you want. Whenever."

"Sure." He didn't look sure.

A low buzz came from the coffee table, where Emily's cell phone slowly turned in a circle.

"Oh, boy." She picked up her phone, opened the text, and growled. "No."

"Em?"

"It's John." Emily held her phone out to the side, pulled it back to reread the text, and quickly shook her head. "I can't. Laura's been kidnapped, I just called into work sick for the first time ever, and now John's—" Her phone buzzed again. "He's blowing up my phone."

"Maybe you should answer," Nickie offered.

"*You* called in sick?" Chuck added.

"No and yes. In that order." Emily put her coffee down and walked into the kitchen. Another restrained grunt of frustration followed her.

"She's figuring it out." Nickie looked at her boyfriend and shrugged. "Lot going on right now."

"Obviously."

"Feel better now that you know we're here?"

"Kind of. Not really, though." Chuck popped his lips a few times and stared at the table. "'Cause I know when that thing's ready, you're gonna go chasing after Laura. Which is good. You should. I just won't know what happened until you come back to tell me."

"I'm sorry, babe." Nickie turned toward him and wrapped both arms around his waist. "I promise. After we finish this and put everything back together, fix magic, the whole thing, you won't have to worry about me at all. You don't *have* to now, but I get it."

For a few seconds, he studied her eyes and held her. Then Chuck rolled his eyes and blew out a long breath, puffing out his cheeks. "Okay. I just have to take your word for it, so I'm gonna do that."

"Awesome."

"Is it?"

Nickie stood on her tiptoes and gave him a quick kiss. "Totally."

Emily roared somewhere in the kitchen, then came storming back out to join them. "I'm losing my mind!"

"Okay." Nickie stepped toward her sister and plucked the phone from Emily's hand. "I'm gonna keep this for you. No more phone. No more John. At least not now."

"I thought you liked John," Chuck said.

"I *do*. That's the problem." Emily watched Nickie slip the cell phone into the pocket of her pajama pants, then vigorously shook her head. Her hands followed, and she jumped up and down a few times. "You're lucky, Chuck."

Nickie's boyfriend let out a halting, confused laugh. "Please keep going. I'd love to hear your reasoning for that."

Nickie slapped his arm with the back of her hand and shot him a joking scowl. "You're lucky enough with me, buddy. Don't forget that."

"Never." The smile he shot her this time was genuine, then he gestured at Emily. "I don't think she was talking about you and me."

Emily scoffed. "Of course not. I'm talking about the whole Peabrain thing. I mean, sure, you haven't *woke up*, yet, but this has to be pretty weird. At least you were with Nickie when you found out about magic."

"Lucky because that thing tried to kill me? Us?"

"No, Chuck." Emily rolled her eyes. "Lucky because when that happened, you weren't in the middle of a park at night with a giant Velikan Engineer stomping around and a bunch of Huldus trying to pick up after her. You got to keep your memories. We got to tell you about who we are. And this mess. John doesn't remember anything."

Chuck shrugged. "Maybe that's not such a bad thing."

"For *him*. Maybe. But *I* remember, and I can't act like everything's okay and normal and zero problems. It was easy to lie to him when I *knew* he didn't know, but I'm gonna let something slip. I'm gonna forget that gnome wiped his memory, and I'm gonna say something stupid like, 'Hey, remember that time we tried to have a nice date, and I ended up talking to a Velikan who built this place?' I know I'm gonna screw it up, and I'm trying to avoid that for as long as possible."

"If you keep blowing him off long enough, Em, that might happen anyway."

Emily sighed. "Just keep my phone away from me right now. As far as everyone else knows, I'm upstairs hurling my guts out."

"Gross."

"Thanks, Chuck."

After righting the chairs around the dining room table, the Hadstrom sisters and Chuck sat around the table and didn't say much as they watched Emily's potion.

Emily stuck her elbows on the table and put her chin in her hands. "I hate waiting."

"I don't know anyone who likes it." Chuck blinked at the Pyrex dish of potion and Laura's graduation gown. "What kinda change are we looking for?"

"The kind that's unmistakable because that's how we find Laura." Emily squished her cheeks in her hands and groaned.

The front door opened much more slowly this time, followed by a polite knock. "Hey, guys," Nathan called, then shut the door.

"Dining room," Nickie said.

The professor stepped quickly through the foyer to join them and stopped. "Hey, Chuck."

"Dude, I know you told me they were okay, but I had to come over anyway."

"I don't blame you." Nathan found an empty chair at the table and sat. "Anything?"

"No." Emily sat back in the chair and folded her arm. "Not even a *little* bit of change."

"Okay, well, we hit the eight-hour mark at nine-thirty, so we still have half an hour. Almost."

Nickie pulled Emily's phone out of her pocket to check the time. "You're ridiculously punctual."

Nathan shrugged. "When it's important? Yeah."

Emily's phone buzzed three times in quick succession, and Nickie almost dropped the thing on the table. "Jeeze."

"John again?" Emily asked.

"Yep. You can't keep him in the dark like this for much longer."

"I *know*." Emily dropped her head back and stared with wide eyes at the ceiling. "Just, one thing at a time."

Nickie put the phone away and crossed one leg over the other. "So, if this doesn't work…"

"It's gonna work." Emily clenched her eyes shut. "It has to."

"We'll go right to the library and look for those clues," Nickie finished. "Or I could just go now if you want. Save us some time, maybe."

"You think you can find the right potions by yourself?" Emily raised her eyebrows.

"Uh, probably not."

"That's what I thought. This'll work. Just another half an hour." With a deep breath, Emily gripped the edge of the table and leaned forward until the underside of her nose rested on the polished wood. "Then we go get her."

CHAPTER NINE

"It's not working!" Emily stood abruptly, pushing her chair out behind her, and stormed out of the dining room.

"It's only nine thirty-five, Em." Nickie glanced at the guys, then stood to follow her sister. "Maybe it's not exact."

"It's a *recipe*, Nickie." Emily stopped in the foyer and faced the stairs. "If it says it takes eight hours, it takes eight hours. Except for it doesn't because we don't have our tracker."

Nickie hurried toward the foyer and waved Chuck and Nathan forward with her. "Might wanna hurry, guys."

After looking quickly at each other, the guys stood and half-jogged into the foyer. The rumbling shift of the Hadstrom sisters' rearranging house built around them. Chuck yelped and jumped into the foyer just before the wall sliding toward the front of the house blocked him from getting in.

"That could really hurt someone," he muttered. "That ever happen?"

"Not yet." Emily stared at the staircase, which now folded on itself like an accordion and dropped into the floor. A few other walls flashed by as they crumpled and dropped, slid into place, and unfolded from the ceiling.

Chuck's mouth popped open as he stared at the undulating ceiling. "This is always gonna be weird."

Nickie grabbed his hand. "You'll get used to it."

"I dunno."

"Em, where are we going?"

The walls finally stopped moving around them, and they stood facing a dinged-up wooden door.

"Huh." A frown flickered across Emily's brow. "Have you seen this one before?"

Nickie shook her head. "Nope."

"That doesn't sound like a good thing," Chuck added.

"What? A room in our house that we've never seen in the two years we've lived here?" Emily shot him a dismissive glance, her mouth turned down in forced calm. "Nah. Can't be a bad thing."

"Where were you *trying* to go?" Nickie asked.

"Wherever Gilroy is right now."

A choked-off laugh came from Nathan. "Who's Gilroy?"

"The rudest magical encyclopedia you'll ever meet." Emily wiggled her eyebrows at him, then stepped toward the wooden door. "You just need a thick skin is all. He doesn't bite."

She opened the door and stepped through slowly, gazing with wide eyes at the new and unknown destination the house had led them to—the house she and her sisters had charmed to rearrange itself like this in the first place. The others followed her through, and they all stopped to take a look at the place.

"Woah." Nickie slipped her hand out of Chuck's and stepped up to nudge her sister. "How is this possible?"

"I have no idea."

"I might be wrong," Nathan said, "but I'm pretty sure this isn't part of your house."

"You're not wrong, Nate." Emily cocked her head and stared at the sloping hillside in front of them. There were huge live oaks spreading their branches out and up, clumps of grandfather moss dangling from them like hair, a bright blue sky overhead, the heat of Austin in the summer, and gravestones dotting the ground as far as they could see.

Chuck turned around and pointed at the open door suspended in midair behind them. "That's gonna stay open, right?"

"It should." Nickie picked up a rock and set it just inside the open door. "But I know where we are."

"I know a cemetery when I see one, babe."

"This one's special, though." Emily made her way down the hill toward the headstone she knew very well beneath the sprawling branches of a live oak that looked older than the others. "I didn't know Gilroy could get out of the house."

"I didn't know everything about this situation." Nickie waved for the guys to follow, and they all headed toward the live oak at the bottom of the small hill.

The cemetery was empty at 9:30 on a Wednesday morning at the end of May. Emily pulled her hair away from her face and neck, which was already covered in a sheen of sweat from the mugginess. The shade under the live oak felt a lot better, even though it only took them two minutes to get there. And right beside the two gravestones the Hadstrom sisters had visited more times than they could count was Gilroy the talking bust.

"How'd you get all the way out here?" Emily asked.

The bust was turned away from her, toward the headstones. Gilroy made no move to turn around and spit his usual insults. Choking, gasping sounds escaped him, and the Hadstrom sisters shot each other confused looks before stepping up beside the marble pillar that held Gilroy off the ground.

"You've been watching our family move through generations for…I mean, probably forever," Nickie said, stopping beside her sister. "Didn't peg you for the sentimental type, though, Gil."

More choking sounds escaped the bust, followed by a few soft scattered thumps onto the green grass beneath the tree. "Neither did I."

Emily's eyes widened. "Gilroy. Are you crying?"

The marble pillar rumbled as the platform at the top turned slowly to face the Hadstrom sisters. Gilroy's stone hair stood on end, and his colorless eyes even duller than usual. There were new wrinkles under his eyes, which were somehow squeezing out tiny pebbles as the once-snarky vault of magical knowledge sobbed openly. The stone tears pattered to the ground. Nickie looked down and saw that he'd already cried a little pile there under the tree.

Emily felt her mouth fall open. "What is this madness?"

Gilroy sniveled, tried to hold his fake breath, and broke into a sob. "I can't answer that question," he wailed.

"Woah, okay." Nickie glanced around the cemetery, but as far as she could tell, they weren't in danger of being found out by any unwoke Peabrains out for a sweltering stroll through the headstones. "Can you still, you know, *answer* questions?"

The talking bust's loud, forceful sniff sounded like tiny rocks rattling inside a tin can.

Just behind the sisters, Chuck leaned toward Nathan and muttered, "That's a statue."

"Yep." Nathan cocked his head.

"That's a talking statue with a name. And it's crying. Pebbles."

"Yep."

"Did you know that was a thing?"

Nathan glanced down at him and raised an eyebrow. "Not like this, no."

"You think you can handle a talk?" Emily asked the bust. "I mean, this is a surprise, but we came looking for you for a reason."

"I probably won't be much help." Gilroy sniffed again and turned on the platform just enough so he could glance back and forth between the Hadstrom sisters and the headstone in front of him. "I never am."

"So, when you're feeling bad about yourself, you come all the way out here to visit Grandma Eloise?" Emily gestured toward the headstone with Eloise Hadstrom engraved on it. "How did you get out of the house?"

"I can do whatever I want, Emily." Gilroy's eyes rolled, and a distraught sigh escaped him. "And this is the only thing I could think of. I just can't stop crying." The last word burst out of him, followed by a much heavier outpouring of tiny pebbles.

Emily glanced at her sister and murmured, "This is nuts."

"Magic, Em." Nickie shrugged. "Finally got to him too."

"That's exactly what it is," Gilroy wailed again. "I don't blame you. Either of you. It's gotta be so *hard* trying to put everything back together again. And you can't even use your magic." He sniffed again, blubbered a little, then continued, "I tried to blame Laura, but now she's… Laura's…"

Emily leaned away as the bust sobbed. Then she made a decision and snapped her fingers in his face. "Okay. Gilroy. Cut it out."

"Easy for *you* to say. You're not feeling emotions for the first time in your existence."

"This is getting way too existential for me," Nickie commented.

"Yeah, for all of us." Emily snapped her fingers in Gilroy's face again. He didn't seem to notice, so she clapped her hands a few times. The pebbles just poured in a new wave from his stone eyes. "Oh, *come on*." She didn't think twice about slapping the bust upside the head, and the shock of it brought his sobbing to an abrupt halt.

"You just hit me." He sniveled and looked up at her with blank gray eyes. "That was…"

"It looks like that was what you needed, Gil." The youngest Hadstrom sister stuck a finger in his face. "We need your help, like always. And now's pretty much the most important time ever for you to buck up and give us the answers we need."

"Buck up?" Gilroy blinked. "That's not even possible. What do you want?"

"You obviously know Laura's been taken," Nickie said. "Where did the gorafrex take her?"

"Lots of places." Gilroy's head drooped on his stone neck, but he only had so much mobility. "She could be anywhere by now."

"What's that supposed to mean?"

"It means I don't know, okay?" More choking sounds escaped the bust, and he stared at their grandma's headstone. "I knew where she was until midnight. Then she just disappeared."

"Okay, you can't say stuff like that, Gil." Emily swallowed hard and fought not to let her emotions take over. Not here. "What happened to her? Did she—"

"She's still alive, if that's what you're worried about." A few more pebbles tumbled down his stone face. "But that thing's hiding her, and I just don't know."

"Hiding her?"

"Not with magic, obviously." Gilroy's head wobbled, and he made a disgusted face at nothing without looking at either of the sisters. "Magic isn't even... It's not... It's broken, and I'm broken, and I don't know what the point of my existence is any more." A much louder, shrieking wail escaped the bust, and pebbles sprang from his eyes in short arcs before hitting the ground.

"Oh, boy." Nickie sighed. "I think that might be all we're gonna get out of him, Em. He's obviously lost it."

"Yeah." Emily looked up from her grandmother's name etched in the headstone and turned toward the bust again. "The gorafrex hid Laura *without* magic?"

"Uh-huh." Gilroy sniffed.

"Okay, Gil. Last question. This is super-important."

"I can't handle anything important right now."

"You want me to slap you again?"

That stopped the talking bust short, and he blinked at her. "No."

"So pull yourself together and answer one more question. Then we'll leave you to mourn the sudden appearance of your feelings in peace." Emily glanced quickly at Nickie and winked. "Would you put potions and alchemy under the same umbrella as magic?"

Gilroy scoffed and looked away from her. "*That's* what's important to you? Are you kidding me?"

"That sounds more like him," Nickie muttered and folded her arms.

"Answer the question, Gil."

"Of *course*, it doesn't fall under magic. That's the most ridiculous thing I've ever heard. But all your questions are ridiculous, aren't they?" Gilroy blinked, startled by the sudden return of his attitude. Then he broke down into rocky tears again.

"Good work." Emily patted the top of the bust's head, which made him wail even louder. Retracting her hand, she turned around and nodded at Nickie and the guys. "Time to go. Don't worry, Gil. We'll fix this, and you'll be back to your sarcastic, biting, crotchety old self before you know it."

"But I know *everything*," he sobbed.

As Emily passed her, Nickie turned to follow her sister, then glanced back at the bust. "Should we just leave him here?"

"He found his way out of the house. He'll find his way back in. I'm pretty sure that blubbering bust doesn't want anyone else seeing him like that. Come on." Emily waved them all up the hill again.

Nathan cleared his throat and hurried after her. Chuck slipped his hand into Nickie's and walked silently beside her toward the open door hanging in mid-air. "So, I didn't understand any of what just happened."

Nickie snorted.

"But Emily looks a lot like she has a new plan."

"Yeah, I know." When they reached the top of the hill, Emily and Nathan were waiting for them. "Okay, Em. You obviously got something out of all that nonsense."

"Yep." Emily stepped through the door and pulled it open to usher the others back into the foyer of the house on Pressler Street. "Potions are not magic. Technically. And magic doesn't work at all right now, so Gilroy can't use it to see Laura."

Nickie opened her mouth and took a deep breath, then closed it again. "Help me out here."

Emily shut the door behind her sister after she and Chuck stepped back into the house. Then she turned around to face them and gave them all that mad-scientist grin that meant she had something really good. "Apparently, the gorafrex considers itself something of an alchemist. But I'm better."

CHAPTER TEN

"Potions." Nickie sighed as the walls and staircase and multiple ceilings shifted around them with that loud, grating rumble. "That actually makes a lot of sense."

"Yep." The house stopped shifting finally, and the last wall slid away to allow them into the dining room again. "Too much sense. I can't believe I didn't think of this before. I mean, you haven't heard the drums since that thing took Laura. And it's not like the gorafrex would just sit around with our sister, not doing anything but hoping magic will somehow turn back on again." She brushed past Chuck and tapped him on the shoulder. He started and looked down to blink at her. "It's not gonna move anymore, Chuck. You're good."

"Okay."

"Wait. To hide Laura from *Gilroy* would take a lot of potions."

"Yep." Emily went to the dining room table and looked at her supplies. "A lot of potions. A lot of different wards and charms to mix up and splatter all over…wherever they are."

Nickie stopped behind the chair next to her sister and folded her arms. "You said that like you know where they are."

"I have a pretty good idea." Emily finished inventorying the vials and jars on the table, then gave Nickie her full attention. "There's only one place that I know of to get all the ingredients anyone would need for that much potions work. Okay, maybe two places, but we know the gorafrex didn't get into Laura's closet."

Nathan shivered. Chuck shot the guy a questioning look, and the physics professor just said, "Don't ask."

"Okay. So the gorafrex…what?" Nickie spread her arms. "Just stopped by the place to pay for a bunch of ingredients? I don't think that thing cares about money, Em."

Emily spun around and scoffed. "I know that. It doesn't make any sense until you add the part about the singing bowl going berserk on us. Twice."

"We didn't see anyone in the park. Just a pig."

"A *pig*?" Chuck snorted. "That's weird."

"You have no idea."

"I mean the *first* time, Nickie." The youngest Hadstrom sister laughed and hurried around the table to grab her mug of coffee. She chugged the whole thing in a few seconds, then slammed the mug down on the table again and stared at Nickie with wide, expectant eyes. "That bowl was doing everything it was supposed to do. It just got confused."

"Oh!" Nickie's eyes popped open, and a smile flickered at the corners of her mouth. "*No.*"

"Oh, *yes.*" Emily nodded vigorously and licked her lips. "Let's go. We have a bunch of other potions to look up now. But this time, I know what we're up against."

"Yeah, right behind you." Nickie headed out of the dining room again, pausing long enough to grab Chuck and plant a kiss on him. "We got this."

"Okay…"

"Hey," Nathan called after them. "Wanna let me know where we're going?"

Emily spun around in front of the door. "*You*, my fine physics-professor friend, get to stay here with Chuck and watch that ceremonial dress in case it starts to work the way I wanted it to. Call us if it does. Nickie has both our phones."

Nathan puffed out a sigh. "Yeah, I can do that. Just, can you at least fill in the blanks first?"

Emily held the door open for her sister, and once Nickie had stepped outside, the youngest Hadstrom sister grinned at the unawakened Peabrain and the professor in her dining room. "The gorafrex holed up in the one place with an endless supply of stuff to keep its potions working."

"You mean, an apothecary."

"That *would* make a lotta sense, huh? We'll be back." Emily slipped outside onto the small porch and closed the door behind her.

Chuck ruffled his blond hair and shook his head. "Every time. They disappear with the worst explanations ever."

"That's what makes 'em so fun, though, right?" It sounded like a joke, but Nathan's lips were pressed tightly together beneath his frown. He clapped Chuck on the shoulder and nodded. "If those two are so sure about this, I'm gonna go with it."

"Right." Chuck stared at the door, wishing he had something better to offer than a bunch of unanswered questions. Then he realized he was standing halfway in the foyer and jumped quickly back into the dining room, searching the ceiling and the walls for movement. "The house with moving walls."

Nickie and Emily parked outside Austin's main library and made their way to the front entrance. "Jeeze, it got hot fast." Nickie drew her hair away from her face and let it fall down her back again.

"Always does." Emily opened the door and waved her sister inside. "Libraries save the day again. With air conditioning."

The library, though, seemed particularly empty at just after ten in the morning. The Hadstrom sisters moved swiftly toward the back of the building, their attention focused on the wall where magicals could easily slip into and out of the restricted section. At least, they used to be able to.

When they stopped in front of the wall, Emily put her hands on her hips. "What the heck?"

"That's new."

"I didn't think you could tack a poster to a wall that

doesn't exist." Emily reached out and carefully poked the cat poster with the words Look Before You Leap in a bold font. The kitten dangling from a tree branch looked terrified. "It's solid. Okay."

"We can still get in, right?"

"We'd better be able to." Emily turned toward the checkout desk on the other side of the walkway and saw the fairy librarian named Isabelle sitting there. The minute she met the young witch's gaze, Isabelle stood from her chair and glanced around the mostly empty building.

"I'm surprised you came back after last time," the fairy said with a tired smile.

"What?" Emily chuckled. "You were incredibly helpful. I found everything I needed. I'm back for more."

Isabelle dipped her head. "Well, I hope your visit today is as successful as your last. Though I doubt it will be."

"What happened?"

"You saw the poster." The fairy nodded at the wall.

"Yeah, I didn't think it was possible to hang anything on that wall," Nickie added.

"Oh, it shouldn't be." Isabelle gave them an uncertain smile. "But many things have changed like that in the last few days. We had to put that poster up to warn people about the issue. Discretely, of course."

"Not very discrete when that wall's been blank for my entire life." Emily stared at the cat poster. "And now it's not working."

The librarian nodded. "It spends most of its time in a solid state now. As far as I know, everyone made it out before that happened. There's maybe, oh, two hours a day altogether where it works the way it should. I'm honestly more concerned about what magic's been doing to the restricted section and all the books."

"Huh." Emily turned around to face the woman. "Well, everything I need right now is in that room. And I don't mean just creature comforts like magic working again for anything. This is more of a life or death situation."

With wide eyes, Isabelle glanced from one Hadstrom sister to the other. "I understand, and I'm sorry that it's come to that for you, whatever the situation may be."

"Thanks. So, can we get inside?"

"Oh." The librarian blinked rapidly and gestured at the wall. "Be my guest. It's not off-limits by any means. We can't keep people from pursuing knowledge, can we? This is a library. I've just been calling this more of an advisory, you know? 'Enter at your own peril' and all that."

Emily fought back a laugh. "Does that turn people away?"

"So far? Yes. At least today. No one wants to get stuck with a bunch of old magical texts and no assurance that they can come back out when they need to."

"Can't blame them." Nickie shot her sister a pointed look. "Em, are you sure this is—"

"Thanks for the warning, Isabelle." Emily set a hand on Nickie's shoulder and spun her older sister toward the wall. "We have a few tricks up our sleeves. Magical and otherwise."

"Good luck." The librarian stepped back with wide eyes to watch the Hadstrom sisters' next move.

"Seriously," Nickie muttered from the side of her mouth. "No reassurance that we'll come back out when we need to? That's not something we can afford to ignore right now."

"I totally agree." Grabbing her sister's wrist, Emily slapped her hand on the wall that should have let her pass right through and grinned. "But we have jumper cables, remember?"

She winked, and both sisters' legacy rings gave off a low pulse of light. Emily pressed a little harder, and then she was stumbling through the warded walls into the library's magical restricted section, dragging Nickie with her.

They barely managed not to fall flat on their faces in the room beyond. Nickie's wrist slipped from Emily's limp fingers and thumped against the older witch's thigh. The Hadstrom sisters stared at what had become of the restricted section. Emily's jaw dropped.

"This is definitely not what I expected."

"Can't expect anything right now, can we, Em?"

CHAPTER ELEVEN

The magical restricted section of Austin's main library had completely come undone. Books floated through the air, some of them flapping open and closed, as if their covers were wings. Others whizzed in all directions with no apparent rhyme or reason as to where they were headed or why. The large worktables placed in the center of the room were warped, half of them bending in arches like plain, dull rainbows while the rest of them looked more like halfpipes. None of the labels for any of the content sections were legible because the letters kept trembling and rearranging themselves. A few had letters in a different language or letters that didn't exist in the original label, or even a few symbols.

"So, why is this place more affected than, say, the park? Or the Mean-Eyed Cat?"

Nickie could only look at her sister for a brief second before she had to duck an incoming book with the image of a whale with wings on the cover. "Have you been to the Mean-Eyed Cat recently, Em?"

"Not since the last time we had our illuminating family meeting."

"Then I wouldn't rule out the craziness there just yet, either."

Emily let out a high-pitched laugh and watched half a dozen books fall from the air to stack themselves perfectly on the ground. The next second, the stack exploded again, and the books shot around the room. "That place is always crazy. Just not like this."

"There's a lot of magic keeping this restricted section together, Em. At least, there *was*. Now it's all—"

"Lost its mind." Emily turned toward the corner on her right, just to the right of the window looking out over downtown Austin, and put her hands on her hips again. "So, we have to go through all these to find the clues from our Hadstrom ancestors, huh?"

"Not all of them. Just the potions books."

"Nickie." The youngest Hadstrom sister pointed at the section of shelves with a label that used to read Potions. "There's only one book in that section."

The single volume that hadn't broken free to roam around the restricted section with its fellows fluttered where it lay, the cover opening and closing slowly like a clamshell.

"Oh, jeeze." Nickie sidestepped away from two books butting themselves against each other in mid-air like fighting bucks. "Looks like we're in for some literary catch-and-release, huh?"

Emily started to nod, then she froze and grinned. "*Or* you could work your magic here and see what happens."

"Look at this." Nickie gestured to the flying books and

pressed her fingers against her thumb like a mouth snapping shut. "Magic. Doesn't. Work."

"There are all different kinds of magic, Nickie. Like potions. Not *technically* magic. Nobody considers them that anymore. But the right potion used the right way does for us what magic can't do for anyone right now."

Nickie stared blankly at her sister. "Potions are your thing."

"I *know!*" Emily clapped her hands, rubbed them vigorously, and turned around to walk backward across the room. "Hmm. I wonder what *your* non-magic magic could possibly be."

"We're kind of on a time crunch, Emily. Remember our kidnapped sister? It's really not the right time for—oh." Nickie blinked and had to react quickly to bat aside the soft-bound mini-books that looked like cheap pocket calendars out of her face before they fluttered away. "You want me to play music for a room full of books?"

"Hey, it worked for the gorlek, right?" Emily gazed at the fluttering chaos. "Last I checked, none of these have razor-sharp beaks and breathe fire. Hopefully."

Just in case, she reached out and knocked on the closest wooden table bent in an arch.

"Yeah, but the gorlek is a living creature. These are just…"

"They're magical books in a magical room in the back of a mostly non-magical library, Nickie. And don't try to convince me magic isn't alive. That this whole *ship* can't think and feel and react on its own. Think of this whole thing with the gorafrex and the powered energy cores as one big, nasty virus, hopefully contained in Austin still."

Emily shrugged and folded her arms, watching a few of the books trying desperately to settle back into their places on the shelves, which trembled so violently that the books took flight again. "And sticking with that analogy, potions would be something like white blood cells. Your *music,* Nickie? A hefty dose of painkillers."

Nickie couldn't hold back a laugh when her sister winked at her again. "Where did you get that weirdly accurate analogy?"

"Making it up as I go." Emily studied a very large slowly flapping book with leather cover covered in dust. It moved toward her, and she held perfectly still until it was close enough for her reach out and snatch it from the air. The minute she touched it, the book was nothing more than a book. She flipped through the pages, then closed it and studied the cover. "Wow. I had no idea magical yoga was a thing."

"What?"

"I mean, it's called something different I can't even pronounce. But look." She turned the book around to show Nickie the image of a vaguely humanoid shape contorted into an impossible pose. "Magicals in the times of Alexandria were gettin' their vinyasa flow on."

Nickie laughed and shook her head. "That's not what we need."

"Yeah, I know." Emily set the book on the closest shelf, and this time, both the shelf and the tome resting on it stayed still. "Huh. Okay, Nickie. In the interest of hurrying this up as much as possible, give it a try, okay? We could do it, but I *really* don't wanna spend all day catching flying books just to read the titles. And I didn't bring my book-catching net."

"Okay, fine." Nickie shook out her hands and ducked again to avoid the next book plummeting toward her. It sailed over her head, thumped against the now-solid wall, and toppled to the floor, shuddering weakly and spinning in a slow circle. "You know, it sounds weird, but I'm glad Laura's not here right now."

"'Cause she'd be throwing a fit about the mistreatment of books. I know."

"I was thinking more along the lines of her witchy heart that's five sizes too big." Nickie eyed the flailing book on the floor, then stepped aside again. "Laura would feel responsible for these books. And I bet she'd start thinking of them as thinking, feeling creatures too if she saw them like this."

Emily barked a laugh. "She'd totally take it on. A menagerie of mad magical creatures *and* a whole rookery of restricted books. No way would she be able to get them past the wards." She nodded at the solid wall beside her sister, then cocked her head. "Except those wards probably don't work right now."

Nickie shrugged. "Yep. Okay, so are we gonna do this thing, or what?"

"It's all you, sis." Emily spread her arms and leaned against the curve of the warped table beside her.

"Of course, I didn't bring a guitar into the library." Nickie cleared her throat, closed her eyes, and took a deep breath. *Just a different kind of magic. And hopefully one that isn't affected by our little energy core oversight.*

She started humming a low, slow tune that came out of

nowhere and didn't belong to any song she knew. The black legacy ring on her thumb pulsed with a warmth she hadn't felt before, but she let it do its thing and hoped her sister was right. Her voice grew a little louder, something whipped through the air, and Emily took in a sharp breath.

"Watch it—"

"Ow!" Nickie's eyes flew open, and she reeled back away from the fluttering book that had tried to close around her face. She batted it aside. "This isn't working."

"That's not a hundred percent true." Emily pointed at the books in the air, which had down their scattered, chaotic trajectories.

Nickie squinted at the change and pursed her lips. "Not like I want to be connected to anyone at the hip, but maybe this would go faster if we…"

"Yep." Emily moved quickly across the room, ducking under the bobbing books and their slowly fluttering pages. When she reached her sister, she set a hand on Nickie's arm and nodded. "Backup boost comin' atcha."

"Try again."

"Sister cables hooked up."

"Em."

"What? You want something boring? 'I have attached my magical abilities to yours, dear sister. Perform your musical routine. I shall fuel your song with my—'"

Nickie slapped her sister's thigh with the back of a hand. "Cut it out."

Emily snorted a laugh and pressed her lips together.

When the older Hadstrom sister picked up her humming melody again, she didn't close her eyes. She just let the song build inside her however it wanted, directed by her intention to get these flying books back where they belonged. The legacy ring on Nickie's thumb grew warmer by the second as the witch's voice rose in volume.

Emily glanced at her own legacy ring and saw it pulsing in rhythm with her sister's humming.

The books fell in line as they flapped through the air, slowly now, and started to settle into something resembling order. They formed a loose circle in the room, with a few stragglers above and below. Nickie kept singing, and as the books flew around, a few of them dropped to the ground beside certain bookshelves. Not a single one settled back onto the shelves, but in under a minute, hundreds of magical tomes from the Library of Alexandria lay in thick piles by the bookshelves.

The last wayward volume flapped erratically, swaying from side to side between two of the visibly separated book piles. Finally, it stopped halfway between them, snapped shut, and thumped to the floor in a pile all its own.

Nickie stopped humming, and the Hadstrom sisters stood there in the sudden silence of the restricted section, waiting for an unexpected reaction.

"All *right*." Emily squeezed her sister's shoulder and shook it a little, then released her and stepped toward the center of the room again. "The library staff will have to fix the tables, but you got the flock of magic-related texts to chill out."

Nickie smiled and shook her head. "For now. Good thinking, Em."

"Uh, thanks. Hey, you should remember this in case I'm too busy to do the thinking for both of us, huh?" Shooting her sister two thumbs-up, Emily turned toward the bulky pile of fallen books in front of what had been the potions section. She bent to pick up the book at the top of the pile and studied the cover. "*Potions for Introverts.* Nice. Looks like they re-organized themselves too."

Nickie grabbed a book from the pile beside her —*Magical Creature Relevance.* A quick glance at the rest of the pile showed a similar theme. "Okay, then. So those are all the potions books over there?"

"Oh, yeah." Emily rifled through the pages of *Potions for Introverts* and shook her head. "But we're looking for notes written onto the pages, right?"

"According to Dad."

Emily stuck the book on the empty shelf behind her, which didn't knock the thing back onto the floor again. "You think Isabelle will be upset if we put the books back in whatever order?"

"The restricted section barely works, Em. But the books aren't flying around and attacking everything that moves anymore, and they're organized by subject. Nobody asked us to do this, and I'm pretty sure nobody would ask for more."

"Good point. Let's get to work." Emily quickly stacked a large pile of books in her arms and brought them to one of the warped tables. "Oh. Right."

"The floor works." Nickie did the same and joined her sister, lowering herself to the floor and plopping down the first stack of books. When she felt Em's grin, Nickie glanced slowly up and widened her eyes. "What?"

"Okay, so you didn't go to college, and you never wanted to. I just have to comment on the fact that there would've been a lot of *this* if you'd gone to college."

Nickie snorted. "A lot of singing magical books into complacency?"

"A lot of sitting on the library floor looking through every book in front of you with absolutely no idea what you're trying to find."

"That doesn't sound even remotely fun."

"Except to Laura, probably."

They both chuckled softly at that, but the mention of their sister sobered them up enough to get to work.

Half an hour and half a dozen books each later, the Hadstrom sisters still sat on the floor in the restricted section, bent low over the vast array of potions recipes in front of them. Emily blew the stray hair out of her eyes and shook her head. "There is a potion for everything."

"It makes sense, if that's what's left when magic takes a day off." Nickie shrugged. "Or a week off."

"Look at this. *Organizing Your Personal Apothecary. Types of Mixing Bowls.* They spell all this stuff out, beginning to end. You know, I bet if an unawakened Peabrain got their hands on one of these, they'd be able to make it work, no problem. And then they'd think they were doing magic without having any idea of what they are." Emily flipped urgently through the last few pages of the book in her lap before setting it back on the shelf beside her.

Nickie blinked at *The Alchemist's Guide to Completing the Home* and went over her sister's words again. "Like Chuck."

Emily snorted. "Well, yeah. I mean, he already knows what he is. Firsthand experience dating a Hadstrom witch and all. So maybe it'd be even better for him. Oh." When the sisters looked at each other, Emily's eyes widened. "Are you cooking up some kinda plan to give your boyfriend a magic-related job?"

"Just a thought, Em." Nickie returned her attention to the book and skimmed through the pages, looking for written notes. "It might get him to calm down if he has something to do that he knows will help us. I'll bring it up."

"That could go either way. Chuck's been really cool about everything. You think he can handle the pressure?"

"He can handle it." Nickie grabbed another book and absently skimmed through the pages, unable to focus on what she was looking for. "Seriously, Em. Don't say anything to him about it until I've had a chance to talk to him first. I still wanna—"

"Stop." Emily pointed at Nickie's next book. "Go back."

"What? This is just a bunch of…" When the older witch checked the cover, she frowned. "*Everyday Love Potions.* I don't think that's anything we can use. I should've checked the cover."

Nickie had lifted the book toward the shelf again, but Emily snatched it from her hand and opened it quickly. "Yeah, love potions don't have anything to do with the gorafrex and family legacies and escape pods, but we're not searching for subject matter, Nickie."

The pages flew through Emily's fingers, then she stopped abruptly and turned back two yellowed leaves of paper. Her finger thumped down onto the top left margin of the right-hand page, and she grinned.

"You weren't looking for the notes, Nickie."

"You found one." Nickie's smile broke through her

distraction. "I really hope that's not just some random kid scribbling in there for fun."

"It's not." Emily skimmed the note's small, neat cursive. "This is definitely for us. Listen. 'Their strength lies in the common bond of their source, both for all three talismans and for the prison they were meant to protect. Cut from a single vein of iron running beneath the surface of the guarded door.'"

"Woah." Nickie leaned forward to glance at the note in the book. "That has to be about our rings and the gorafrex prison, right? What else could that refer to?"

"Good thing we're not trying to find out." Emily ran her finger over the densely scrawled message and stopped. "Whoever wrote this note signed it. L.H."

"H for Hadstrom."

"I'm willing to take that bet." Emily flipped through one more page and stopped to read the note in the same hand at the bottom. "Oh, man."

"Okay, I can't read upside down, Em."

Shooting her sister a mischievous grin, Emily widened her eyes and felt as on the verge of madness as she looked. "Dad was right. Clues left for us in the restricted magic books."

"What's it say?"

"'Seek the ones who took their purpose underground. Chapter seven.' And they underlined a reference to *Alchemy of the Bronze Age.*"

"Great." Nickie ran a hand through her hair and scanned the massive pile of books between them. "So, we still have to go through the rest."

"Phone." Emily held out her hand and waited for her

sister to hand over her cell phone. She ignored the twelve unread texts from John and opened the camera to take pictures of the most important pages in *Everyday Love Potions*, at least for her and her sisters. *And maybe a little ironic.*

Then she flipped through the rest of the pages to be sure there weren't any other notes, and finally set the book back on the shelf. "We need to send Dad a thank you basket or something."

"Seriously?" Nickie laughed. "Yeah, thanks for helping us save the world, Dad. Here's some chocolate-covered fruit."

"Hey, it's the thought that counts." A victorious laugh burst from the youngest Hadstrom sister's mouth, and she picked up another book from the pile with renewed energy. "Our ancestors set us on a freakin' treasure hunt!"

CHAPTER TWELVE

When Nickie pulled up to the curb in front of their house on Pressler Street, Emily unbuckled her seatbelt, whipped open the door, and slammed it shut after jumping out onto the sidewalk.

"Hey." Nickie was close behind her, sticking her keys in her back pocket. "Your car might be able to take a beating, Em. I'd like to keep mine working as long as possible."

"Sorry." Emily hurried up the stairs, shaking out her hands and trying not to explode with excitement. "I'll treat it like glass next time, okay?"

"That's not what I'm… Never mind." Nickie followed her sister up the stairs and the cement walkway to the tiny front porch.

Emily almost threw the front door open and stopped just inside the foyer. "Oh. You're still here. Awesome."

Nathan and Chuck stood from their chairs at the dining room table, sharing a confused glance as Emily headed straight for her collection of ingredients spread out beside the potion she'd made the night before.

"Find anything?" Chuck asked.

"Yeah, a gold mine." The youngest Hadstrom sister took out her phone—which had buzzed with new texts the whole drive back from the man library—and opened the dozens of photos she'd taken of all the notes they'd managed to find from one Hadstrom ancestor or another. "We need to go hunting for an iron mine. I think."

The guys turned to Nickie, who shut the front door behind her and stepped into the dining room with a shrug. "I can't tell if she's actually on to something or if this is just residual shock."

"Shock?" Chuck swallowed.

"I'm fine." Emily laughed. "I had to at least *try*. It would've saved us a lot more time than having to go all the way back to the library if we missed any of these clues. Notes. Helpful hints."

Nickie fought back a laugh at the matching expressions of complete cluelessness both Nathan and Chuck shot her way. "She tried to take a few potions books home with her."

"*What?*" Nathan blinked at Emily. "Why would you—"

"The whole restricted section is on the fritz, Nate," Emily said, waving him off as she set aside various potions ingredients for her next endeavor. "Flying books, twisted furniture. The wall barely opens anymore, apparently." When she looked up at the others, all of them were staring at her. She rolled her eyes. "Oh, come on. Don't tell me you wouldn't have tried it too."

"I definitely *wouldn't* have tried it." Nathan folded his arms and couldn't help a smile of disbelief. "I've heard those wards pack a punch."

"Not nearly as much as they're supposed to." Emily rubbed the back of her neck, then pulled her shoulders back and returned to the images on her phone. "Now it's just a little bit of static."

Nickie raised an eyebrow. "Static, Em? You were electrocuted and got your hand stuck in the wall."

"Yeah, and you got me out. I don't see the big deal."

Chuck set a hand on Nickie's shoulder and stared blankly at the jars and vials and boxes strewn across the table. "Anyone else want some water?" Nobody answered, so he nodded and turned slowly into the kitchen, muttering, "Electrocuted?"

"The most important thing now is that we know exactly where to go to get this the last piece of a tracking spell I *know* the gorafrex can't counteract. Oh, hey." Emily looked up at Nathan and pointed to Laura's graduation gown, still twisted on the baking sheet. "Anything happen with that thing?"

"Not even a little."

"Well, we can forget that one. It's not nearly as important to Laura as I thought it was."

The physics professor stepped hesitantly up to the table and watched Emily's hands flying rapidly from her phone to the ingredients. "Sounds like you found the best thing to track her with."

"Yep." Emily shot him a thumbs-up, then glanced at her legacy ring. "The rings—hers, mine, Nickie's. A reconstructing potion is a *lot* more powerful than stuffing a baggy dress into a singing bowl. And our rings mean a lot more to us than anything Laura stuck in frames on her wall."

"They mean a lot more to the gorafrex too, Em." Nickie exchanged glances with Nathan and moved closer to her sister. "That thing has to know by now that we have the rings. And it's smart. It's probably working on its own potion right now to mess with the rings."

"Nope." Emily scanned the items she'd gathered, looked at her phone one more time, and nodded. "I need some widowfan. In the greenhouse."

"Hey, hold on a second—"

"The gorafrex isn't gonna touch our rings." The youngest Hadstrom sister turned toward Nickie and spread her arms. "They're made of iron, which is the witch-killer's one and only weakness. And we need to go back to the—"

A fierce knock came at the door, and everyone turned to look at the foyer.

"You guys invite anybody else over?" Nathan asked.

"Unless it's Laura, no." Emily leaned back against the edge of the dining room table, trying to hide the huge mess of her supplies.

"I'll get it." Nathan turned into the foyer and paused briefly at the front door before opening it. "Oh. Hey, John."

"Hey, man. I, uh, is Emily here?"

"Yeah, but I don't know if right now's the best time, man."

Emily went back to the unopened texts on her phone and saw the last one John had sent her.

I want to make sure you're okay. If you don't get back to me by 11, I'm coming over.

"Awesome," she whispered.

Nickie headed into the foyer, grabbing her sister's shirtsleeve to tug Emily along with her.

"Maybe it sounds crazy," John continued on the front porch, "but I keep getting this feeling that something's wrong. Did she say anything about…I dunno, not wanting to talk to me or something?"

"No." Nathan shook his head and shifted his weight, clearing a path for John to see inside.

"Hey." John pushed the door open, and Nathan stepped back to let him inside. "Emily, what's going on?"

She froze and plastered a weak smile onto her face. "*Hi!*"

John looked like he was about to hug her but stopped a few inches away instead. He couldn't decide what to do with his hands and finally settled for rubbing the back of his neck. "I've been texting you all morning."

"Yeah, sorry. I dropped it in the toilet last night. Had to do the whole pan-of-rice-in-the-oven thing."

"What?"

"Dries it out." Emily spread her arms and glanced at her sister. "Everything's okay, though. You didn't need to come over."

"Malino said you called in sick this morning. Said it was really bad, and when you didn't answer, I just…" John stopped, took in the fact that his girlfriend's sister and Nathan were both standing there with them in the foyer, and leaned forward to whisper, "Can we talk alone for a sec?"

"Now's not a good time." Emily wrinkled her nose. "There's a lot going on."

"Okay." He looked her over and frowned. "Are you actually sick?"

"Uh, no." She blinked and paused with her mouth open just long enough to blow all possibility of a convincing lie out of the water. "It's Laura. She caught something really bad, and I thought I was getting it too. But we're just trying to keep her hydrated, and…"

The silence in the foyer was deafening. Chuck stepped out of the kitchen with a full glass of water raised to his lips. When he saw the tense conversation in front of the door, he paused, lowered the glass, and cleared his throat. "Hey, John."

"Chuck."

"Here you go, Em." Chuck walked toward her and handed her the glass. "She need anything else?"

"Nope." Emily plucked the glass from his hand and turned toward the stairs. "Just lots of fluids. Thanks." She moved stiffly toward the stairs and halfway turned back toward John as she climbed. "I'll call you when I have more time."

"I can wait if you—"

"Sorry. Gotta play nurse." Emily hurried up the stairs and headed for Laura's bedroom, where she chugged the entire glass of water and held her breath to listen to the rest of the conversation. *What am I doing?*

"It's really that bad?" John asked, looking from Nathan to Nickie to Chad.

"Might even be a bit of an understatement." Nickie gave him a sympathetic smile and nodded toward the open front door. "I'll make sure she calls you when Laura doesn't need us as much anymore."

John cleared his throat again and nodded. "Yeah, okay. Thanks." He turned back to the door and seemed to reconsider. "Hey, I'm sorry if I crossed a line by coming over."

"Don't be," Nathan said.

"Yeah, we do it all the time." Chuck scratched his head. "I get it. It's hard not to wonder what—"

A high-pitched squeal rose from the dining room table, followed by a few crackling pops and bright-blue sparks flying from Laura's graduation gown on the table.

John tried to peer around the corner into the dining room. "That doesn't sound good."

"Now's not a good time, man." Nathan put a hand on the unawakened Peabrain's shoulder and guided him firmly toward the door. The blue light from the potion pulsed rapidly, lighting up John's baffled frown.

"Issues with the oven, too," Nickie muttered and headed into the dining room.

"We'll let you know when things settle down." Nathan held the door open, and Chuck joined him, blocking John's view of the dining room and the kitchen and the chaos blazing on the table.

"Does this happen a lot?" John shoved his hands into his pockets as all three guys stepped out of the house.

Chuck tried not to stare at what looked like cubes of ice being tossed into the foyer behind them and shut the door. "You mean emergencies and not answering phones? All part of dating one of the Hadstrom sisters."

Nathan stared at him and raised his eyebrows. "You would know."

"Yup. Been like this for years."

"Huh." Just before John turned back for one more

glance at the Hadstrom sisters' house, the pulsing blue light spilling from behind the curtained window in the dining room cut off. "So, Emily hasn't said anything about me, I guess?"

"Not to us." Nathan shrugged.

"Or anyone, probably," Chuck added. "Just how she is."

John chewed his lower lip and nodded. "Okay. I gotta get to work, so please remind her to call me, yeah?"

"No problem."

"You got it."

Shooting the guys a final confused glance, John turned jerkily toward his truck. Nathan and Chuck stood at the top of the stairs until Emily's boyfriend started the engine and took off down Pressler Street. Then Chuck puffed out a sigh and shook his head. "Man. Did *I* look that lost?"

"Before the gorafrex almost killed you and Nickie had to tell you all about magic and their deadly quest to save the ship?" Nathan let out a dry laugh at Chuck's blank expression. "Yep. Just like that."

"Someone's gotta tell him."

"Well, when it's an option, that's up to Emily." The professor turned around and headed back up the walkway toward the front door. "Come on. There's gotta be something they still need us for in there."

Chuck frowned down the street, then followed. "Never thought I'd have to lie about Laura being sick. That was too easy."

CHAPTER THIRTEEN

C huck and Nathan stepped back into the house to see Nickie stomping on a pile of dark fabric between the dining room table and the window. Bright blue smoke rose from Laura's graduation gown in thick pillars, giving the whole room and half the kitchen a hazy blue tinge.

"Woah, babe." Chuck leaned hesitantly forward. "That the best way to put out a magical fire?"

"Oh, ha-ha." Nickie waved the smoke out of her face and stepped off the gown. "It is when the fire wasn't supposed to light in the first place. And when magic is—"

The crumpled gown erupted in blue sparks again, all of which darted toward the front of the house. They singed the living room wall and the curtains drawn over the windows as they passed.

"Are you serious?" Nickie stomped on the gown again, snuffing out the sparks and filling the dining room with more smoke until all three of them were coughing and trying to wave the stuff away.

Emily thumped quickly down the stairs and joined them in the coughing fit. "What did you *do*?"

"Nothing!" Nickie hastily kicked Laura's gown into a pile and stood on it with both feet. The blue smoke lessened into a thin trickle, but she didn't step off. "Your potion worked. I think."

Emily glared at the singed, flattened, dirt-trodden possession Laura had gone through all the trouble to frame on her bedroom wall. A bark of laughter escaped her. "It's *symbolic!*"

Her sister snorted and glanced down at the wreck under her boots. "Think she'll notice?"

"Was it supposed to do that?" Nathan asked.

"Probably not." With a shrug, Emily stepped toward the table and took out her phone again. As she scrolled through her new images of Hadstrom-family notes in restricted-book margins, the dining room fell tensely silent again. She looked up and sighed. "Okay. Just so you guys don't have to keep bottling it all up, I get it. I need to talk to John. Or at least quit ignoring him. Or maybe I'll just tell him everything about magic and what we're doing—"

"Come on, Em!"

"I *know* I can't do that, so I won't." The youngest Hadstrom sister pointed at the others standing in her dining room. "Thanks for covering for me. Good thinking with the water, Chuck." He shot her a thumbs-up and a weak smile. "I'll try not to make anyone lie for me again. I just can't deal with more than finding Laura right now. I don't even want to…"

While Emily clenched her fists, a light flush creeping up along her cheekbones, another few strings of blue smoke puffed from beneath Nickie's boots. "Okay, Em. No problem. Special circumstances and all. But maybe just take a deep breath or try meditation or something, huh? I think whatever emotional thing that was messing with your magic might be finding a new outlet in your potions."

"Oh." Staring at the smoke, Emily approached her sister and grabbed Nickie's wrist. Black and copper legacy rings glowed for a second, and the previously dry, smoking graduation gown sloshed with conjured water. A dirty, ash-filled pool of it spread across the dining room floor beneath Nickie's feet.

"I guess that works." Nickie stepped off the gown and watched it for any more signs of unapproved fireworks. "We need to focus on what we *can* do now."

"Yep." Skimming through her phone again, Emily wrinkled her nose. "I still don't know what 'beneath the gates' means."

"Can I see?" Nathan held out his hand.

"You any good at scavenger hunts?"

The physics professor took Emily's phone with a smirk and scrolled through the pictures. "Not really. I can find a pattern in almost anything, though. Occupational hazard." He stopped, flipped back and forth between two pictures, and looked at the sisters. "Have you guys gone back to the Greenbelt yet?"

Chuck laughed. "I know it's still hot out, man, but swimming probably isn't on the schedule."

Emily bit her lip and shook her head in pity.

"Not swimming, babe," Nickie said. "That's where Laura let the gorafrex out."

"Right. Yeah, I knew that."

"Laura went back there to find the binding rune you helped her put together," Emily told Nathan.

He nodded. "The one on her iron lance."

"Yep. It definitely works." Nickie shrugged. "At least, it binds the gorafrex. Emily didn't get a chance to use her potion for removing the thing from its host, which was the last part we needed to put it back in its prison."

"So, if we can track Laura with whatever potion I make…" Emily nodded at her phone in Nathan's hand.

"Yeah, this is talking about the grounding element. Right up there with the iron vein and 'those who took their purpose underground.'" The physics professor handed Emily her phone again and folded his arms. "If I were you, the first place I'd look is the Greenbelt. Where the entrance to the prison is, for lack of a better phrase, I guess. If your ancestors and the Engineers worked together to built that prison, it makes sense that their rings were made at the same time."

"You mean our legacy rings were cut from the same iron as the gorafrex's prison?" Nickie shook the hair out of her face and caught her sister's gaze.

"That's creepy," Emily muttered. "And it makes so much sense. I like it."

"So, let's go to the Greenbelt."

"Okay, hold on, though. I wanna get this last potion started first." Emily slowly turned toward Chuck and shot him an exaggerated wink. "Okay, Chuck, ol' buddy. I have a job for you."

Nickie's boyfriend laughed with wide eyes. "Very funny."

"No, seriously. We need all the help we can get right

now, and you just happen to be standing in our dining room. You in or what?"

"Wait, you… There's something…" Chuck let out a surprised snort and spread his arms. "Of course I'm in, Em. I thought you'd never ask."

"Awesome." She clapped a hand on his shoulder, which was awkward, seeing as he was a foot taller than her. "I need one more thing from the greenhouse before Nickie and I go check out the Greenbelt."

All the pride and excitement drained from Chuck's face. "Is this is the same greenhouse that turned into a flesh-eating jungle when magic started un-magicking?"

"Yep. Oh! No, I'm not gonna make you go in there." Emily chuckled, set her phone back on the table, and headed into the foyer. "I *do* need Nickie's help with that. We'll get the last ingredient. You guys just make sure everything else in that recipe is here, other than the grounding element and this widowfan. We'll be right back."

Nickie left a quick kiss on Chuck's cheek, gave him a reassuring nod, and followed her sister. "Won't take us long."

"You sure it's safe?" Chuck's voice got a little hoarse at the end, and he cleared his throat.

"Hey, we rearranged the magical restricted section of the library and got the singing bowl to work at one point. Give us a little credit." Emily grinned at the guys as Nickie joined her in the foyer, waving as the house started rumbling and groaning and rearranging around them. "Don't blow anything up before we get back."

Then a wall unfolded from beside the staircase and slid

into place, blocking the sisters off from the Peabrain and the professor in their dining room.

Nickie folded her arms and waited for the house to stop moving. "Okay, admittedly, I love that you're trying to make him feel more included in everything. I'm still hung up on what you're gonna have him do."

"Who, Chuck?" Emily rolled her eyes at her sister's raised eyebrow. "Harmless stuff. We need to save as much time as we can, so while we hike to the creek, Chuck can stay here and make the potion we need. Well, most of it. I won't have to, and he gets to help us. It's a win-win for everybody, right?"

"Just as long as you're sure he won't blow anything up while we're gone."

Emily pressed her lips together and tried to hide a smirk. "That's up to him, Nickie. But I *can* promise that the only dangerous ingredients in this potion are the ones we don't have yet."

"Fine. Just don't give the dangerous ones to Chuck."

"Are you kidding me? I know how that works. It's like letting a kid help you bake cookies."

"What?"

Emily blinked at her sister, and the walls finally slid into place around them to reveal the door to the greenhouse. "The kid can mix all the ingredients and measure and pour and everything, but you don't tell 'em to set the timer or take the cookie sheet out of the oven."

"Only you would make that kind of analogy, Em."

"Thanks." Emily turned the handle on the door and paused to reach for her sister with the other hand. "This gives a whole new meaning to the buddy system, doesn't it?"

"Like holding hands in the parking lot. Don't let go, and magic just might work when you need it." Nickie grabbed her sister's hand, and they stepped into the flesh-eating jungle in their magical greenhouse.

CHAPTER FOURTEEN

"Woah. I didn't think this could get any worse."

Nickie pulled the greenhouse door shut behind her and squeezed Emily's hand. "You weren't kidding."

"You thought I was joking?" Emily stepped carefully over the massive roots protruding from what had once been the greenhouse's tiled floors. Now the tiles were splintered into tiny fragments and covered in roots of all sizes, some of them corkscrewing up into larger plants than the Hadstrom sisters had put there. Vines and thick branches clung to the walls and the ceiling, blocking out most of the light from the glass windows that lined the three outer walls and the ceiling. "Little red flower on the end of a vine, Nickie. Slithered all the way over to Mom's workbench, which apparently isn't there anymore, and tried to eat me."

"Mom's workbench?"

Emily pointed at the pile of rotted wood in the left

corner. "Deteriorated, I guess. Good thing I already took out all her supplies."

"Okay, we're looking for a widowfan, right?"

"Yep." The youngest Hadstrom witch pulled her older sister along, ducking beneath an overhanging bough draped with blue leaves and purple berries covered in nasty-looking black thorns. "It's a kind of fern. Doesn't usually grow in large amounts, and I know we had some at the back of the greenhouse. But who knows? Could be anywhere at this point."

"We didn't plant any of this stuff when we moved in." Nickie reached up to swipe aside the massive fan-shaped leaves in front of her.

"Don't touch those." Emily jerked her sister down by the hand. "Go *under*, Nickie. Just to be safe."

"It's a leaf. How unsafe could it—"

The orange leaf curled at the tip and rolled all the way up to the stalk, emitting an orange cloud of gas that smelled like skunk spray.

"If it stinks, there's a good chance it's not safe." Emily tugged her sister past the reeking leaves and between two large stands of what looked like bamboo coated in dripping slime. "And no, we didn't plant any of these. I think the messed-up magic tried to have a little fun in here. Or maybe this is just another season of *Greenhouse Gone Wild*."

Nickie pulled her foot away from the small tendrils of green and brown roots trying to build a net around her ankle. At the movement, the netted roots jerked back toward the ground to wait for another unsuspecting victim. "It's amazing to me that you can walk through a deadly forest in our house and make jokes at the same time."

"Someone's gotta do it. Oh, right there." Pointing toward a small opening in the thick, carnivorous vegetation, Emily picked up the pace.

Nickie tripped over a fallen log covered in oozing purple fungi and decided to breathe through her nose when the pustules on the gathered mushrooms burst one by one. "Just thinking out loud, Em. Any idea how we're gonna get all this to clear out? You know, when we put magic right again."

"I can't think that far in the future, but we'll figure it out." Emily stopped at the innocuous-looking ferns in the corner, then gazed at the dark, dank, misty jungle around them. "I'm kinda hoping these things will turn on each other and fix the problem for us."

"Yeah, that would be nice."

"Okay. Widowfan. Let's get in here and— Ow!" Emily jerked away from the ferns, which had lashed out against her ankle the second they decided she'd gotten too close.

"Is that supposed to happen?" Nickie asked.

"Nope." Scowling at the offending fern and the splatters of blood dripping off the frond, Emily lowered her voice and whispered, "This is gonna get a little tricky. Don't make any sudden movements, but don't stand still for too long."

"Why are we whispering, Em?"

"Because I'm trying not to freak out." She glanced at the crimson stain around the rip in the bottom of her jeans. "I'm pretty sure they can smell blood."

"You mean the plants."

"Yep. This is the part where we power up the Hadstrom magic, Nickie." Careful not to lean too close to the widowfan, Emily squeezed her sister's hand and pointed at the fern. Both legacy rings flashed, and a bright spark of light shot from Emily's outstretched fingers. Two fern fronds separated from the stalk and dropped to the ruined greenhouse floor. "Great. Now we just—"

"Look out!" Nickie raised her arm to shield them both from the huge moss-covered branch that descended upon them from the above. The moss shrieked and clawed at the air, and Nickie's legacy ring launched a much more powerful version of her sister's pruning spell. Blinding silver light cleaved the branch in two, and the severed half dropped to the ground inches from where Emily squatted.

"Oh, screw it." Emily shot out her hand to grab the two fronds of widowfan for her potion, but she wasn't quick enough to avoid the fern's attack. An onslaught of razor-sharp fronds lashed the young witch's exposed wrist and forearm lightning-quick. More blood splattered against the closest flora, which was a black flower the size of a softball that looked a lot like a panther's head. The flower's jaws clamped down on Emily's blood and let out a low, warning snarl.

Nickie whipped her head toward every rustling branch and descending vine and bursting flower around them, then shouted, "Got it?"

"Let's go!" Emily jumped up from her squat and ran, clinging tightly to the widowfan fronds in one fist and her sister's hand in the other. Two white roots like pale worms shot from the ground in front of them. Emily sidestepped around the first, but the second opened a mouth and clamped down on the toe of Nickie's boot.

"What the—" Nickie tried to shake it off and keep running, but the root held fast, jerking her and Emily back toward him. "Em, it has *teeth*!"

Both sisters' rings aimed a barrage of searing flames at the white root, which instantly released Nickie's boot and writhed across the pieces of broken tile, its outer husk now a black crust.

"Come on!" Emily yanked Nickie forward with her, and the carnivorous plants followed the trail of blood the youngest witch left behind. They ducked under the stands of slimy bamboo that bent toward them with an unnatural groan, and Emily glimpsed the door to the foyer. "Just keep running."

Vines dropped from the ceiling in an apparent attempt to catch the sisters before they could escape. Some coiled around Emily's arm, but Nickie's ring erupted in a bright burst of sparks and yellow light, and the vines dropped to the floor like an upended bucket of snakes.

Just before they reached the door, a six-foot stalk with a blossom the size of a sunflower bent toward them, blocking them off. The red blossom also had teeth, which dripped a thick, green-white substance that left black craters in the destroyed floor. A wail like a crying baby issued from the flower's bright-red center. Emily drew her arm back and sent a killer right hook into the side of the flower with a wet, sickening thump. Half the petals and the acidic green-white sludge sailed toward the other side of the greenhouse, then the door was open, and both witches lurched through it and into the foyer.

Nickie slammed the door shut with an echoing bang as another killer plant thumped against the closed door. The handle rattled and turned a few centimeters back and forth, and a thin puff of yellow gas sprayed under the closed door.

The sisters stared at it, listening to the sounds of the hunger-crazed flora in their accidental jungle, and backed away. Instantly, the house shifted and groaned around them, rumbling into another configuration as the walls receded, doorways spun past, and the staircase finally unraveled itself to its original position. The walls opened back up on both sides of the foyer, and when the house settled again, the only thing anyone could hear was Nickie and Emily's heavy breathing.

Chuck peered around the entryway with wide eyes. "You guys okay?"

"Yeah," Nickie panted.

"Totally fine." Emily squeezed her sister's hand again, then released it and turned toward the dining room. "There's gotta be a magical version of Round-Up somewhere."

"Honestly, Em, that might make it worse." Nickie nudged Emily's shoulder and let out a chuckle of disbelief. "You'd probably get better results if you went in there with a pair of boxing gloves."

They both laughed, and Emily shook out her right wrist, although she didn't let go of the crumpled fronds she'd barely managed to get out of there.

"What..." Nathan's eyes widened when he took in the Hadstrom sisters' appearance: the deep teeth marks surrounded by white powder on Nickie's boot, the slashes across Emily's right pantleg and all up her forearm, and the twigs still wriggling in Emily's dark hair. He pointed to his head. "A little something came back with you."

Emily slapped her head until the twigs clattered to the floor, and she stomped them into a pile of sawdust and orange powder on the floor. Then she shrugged and headed toward the dining room table again. "Time to get to work."

Chuck approached Nickie and looked her over from head to toe. "What happened in there?"

"It's fine." She nodded and tried to wave him off. "I'm fine."

"What about your sister?" Nathan asked, gazing at the bloody slashes on Emily's arm.

"I'm *fine*. The widowfan isn't poisonous or anything. More like stinging nettle, honestly."

"So it hurts."

"Well, yeah." Emily shook her head and eyed the ingredients Nathan and Chuck had set aside for the new potion while the Hadstrom sisters braved the dangers of their greenhouse. "But it'll go away in a bit."

"Okay." Chuck continued to eye them. "It looks like you guys got attacked. Was there something else in there?"

"Nope. Just plants."

Nickie turned to her boyfriend and raised her eyebrows. "Plants that act a lot like animals."

"They're not all bad." Emily dropped the widowfan fronds on the table and wiggled her head. "Okay, maybe even the gentle ones have turned. I would really love to not have to go back in there. Chuck!"

"Yeah." Nickie's boyfriend hurried to her side.

"This is what I want you to do while we go to the Greenbelt, okay?" She pointed at the pictures on her phone. "Put all these things together. Measure just like it says—"

He laughed and tried to cover it with a cough. "I know how to follow a recipe."

She grinned at him and stepped away from the table. "Okay, then. We'll let you get to work. Oh, and don't use the red parts of that widowfan."

"Red parts." Chuck scanned the crumpled fronds on the table, then turned quickly toward the foyer as Nickie and Emily headed toward the front door. "Red parts as in blood?"

"Yep. That's not part of the recipe. I don't wanna know what might happen if a little bit of me got into the potion." Emily shot him a thumbs-up. "You got this, Chuck. I believe in you."

"Yeah, thanks." He hunched his shoulders, rolled them back into place, and nodded at the ingredients. "I got this."

"I'm coming with you guys again," Nathan said.

Chuck whirled away from the table. "*What?*"

"Just like you said, man. You got this." Nathan gave him a reassuring nod and followed the Hadstrom sisters toward the front door.

Nickie blew him a kiss as Emily opened the front door. "Call me if anything that's not supposed to happen happens."

"Not supposed to…" The door closed again, leaving him alone in the Hadstrom sisters' house, and Chuck sighed. "Yeah, I got this." He picked up the first jar, unscrewed the lid, and got to work.

CHAPTER FIFTEEN

"Just out of curiosity," Emily said, turning around in the passenger seat of Nickie's car to eye Nathan in the back, "did you hightail it out of there just to get away from Chuck doing potions, or do you know something we don't?"

"He'll be fine. I didn't wanna distract him. Whoever came up with the idea to let him try his hand with mixing a few things together, I think it's a good idea."

Emily grinned at Nickie and patted her sister's leg. "A good idea."

"I told you the same thing, Em."

"I know. I'm just basking in it." Emily turned back toward Nathan. "The other option is that you know something we don't. Spill it."

"If I *knew* anything, of course, I'd tell you." Nathan glanced at the window and rested his head back on the seat. "Mostly, I don't do very well just sitting around and waiting for things to happen. I could handle it when I knew the three of you were together, but now…"

"Now Laura's somewhere else. We get it." Nickie nodded at him in the rearview mirror but wasn't sure if he saw it. "Thanks for being around to help."

"I mean, it's the middle of summer." Nathan shrugged, his lips twitching in a tiny smile. "My choices are run around with you guys to get her back and fix magic or spend all day in my office unpacking boxes and setting up lesson plans, so…"

Emily snorted. "That sounds *awful.*"

"Comparatively, yeah. And if we're going to the Greenbelt to check out a prison made on this ship by the magicals who *built* the ship, I might have an insight when we least expect it. Who knows?"

"Ah, right." Emily nodded slowly. "The part-Kashgar comes from a long line of Kashgar mechanics. That it?"

"Something like that."

"Help is help." Nickie pulled the sun visor down over the windshield and turned up the AC. "Which is why we're gonna take a little detour first."

"To where?"

"The same place Laura goes whenever she's got some magical digging around to do."

The door to Hopkins Antiques jingled when they stepped inside. Emily wrinkled her nose. "Smells like pennies in here."

"I was gonna go with dust and old books, but okay." Nickie led the way through the antique store and the shelves of magical artifacts, display areas of ridiculously old furniture, and cases of jewelry, knives, and silverware. No one stood behind the counter in the back, so she cleared her throat and tapped the bell. "Hello?"

They waited a few more seconds, then Emily pounded the bell a few times. "Carl! We know you're not busy. There's no one else here."

"Maybe give him a minute, huh?"

"Right, 'cause we have all the time in the world for a leisurely wait."

Carl Hopkins poked his head out of the room in the back, munching on a snack, and his eyes widened when he saw the Hadstrom sisters in his shop. He lifted a finger, then disappeared and came back out with a full cup of tea in his hand.

"Just a second." Carl drained the tea and set it on the counter with a satisfied sigh, then folded his hands and grinned at them. "I'd say I'm happy to see you both, but more than that, I'm curious as to why it's just the two of you."

"Laura's busy," Emily muttered.

"Ah." Carl's gaze fell on the tall professor behind the sisters, and he paused. "And who's this?"

"I'm Nathan." He approached the counter and smiled. "Just came along for the ride."

"Excellent. Carl Hopkins. Happy to meet you." The man stuck his hand out, and Nathan shook it briefly. "Forgive me for mentioning it, but there's something about your..." He gestured to his own eyes.

"That's the Kashgar, Carl," Emily said.

"Part-Kashgar," Nathan corrected, and she shrugged.

"Oh, yes. Thank you." Carl nodded and glanced at the

Hadstrom sisters, waiting. "I take it you came in for a reason?"

"Yep." Nickie leaned forward, though there was no one else in the shop. "We're looking for tools."

When she didn't say anything else, Carl chuckled. "You'll have to be a little more specific."

"*Mining* tools," Emily added.

"Mining?"

"For pure iron." The youngest witch shot him a peppy smile.

"I'm not sure I have anything like that, I'm sorry to say." Carl glanced at Nathan, wondering just how far the Hadstrom sisters were willing to go to pull off a prank like this. "And even if I did, it probably wouldn't do what it's supposed to. Magic isn't doing anyone any favors these days, in case you hadn't heard."

Emily grimaced at the untimely reminder. "Yeah, that part's kinda hard to miss, Carl."

Carl chuckled. "What are you really here for? I'm having a hard time wrapping my head around the idea of Laura Hadstrom's sisters walking around hacking at the ground with picks and digging for iron." A sharp laugh escaped him, and he turned away to hide his smile, flitting a hand at the witches and the man on the other side of his counter. "Sorry. I just… It's a funny image."

"He's making fun of us," Emily muttered.

Nickie set a hand on her sister's shoulder. "Just give me a sec." With a sigh, Emily backed away from the counter and went to study a pile of old rabbit furs next to an intricately carved armoire against the wall. "Carl."

The owner of Hopkins Antiques wiped tears from the

corners of his eyes and sniffed. "I'm not laughing at you. I hope you know that. I just, well, I always assumed there was a reason Laura came in here instead of either of you. Mining for iron, though?" He shook his head and chuckled again. "That's—"

"Exactly what we need," she interrupted. The man blinked at her but didn't seem to get it yet. "We're looking for a very specific vein of iron. Laura's in trouble, and that's the only option we have right now to help her."

Carl choked on his laughter and froze. "She's in trouble?"

"Yeah."

"I…" He glanced around the room, briefly stopping to watch Emily rub her hand over the furs. "Does this trouble by any chance have anything to do with Barton Creek and a certain dagger I sold Laura last month?"

Nickie bit her lip and nodded. "I'm not too sure about a dagger, but it's definitely a Barton Creek kind of problem."

Carl's eyes darted toward Nathan. "You don't have to say anything else, Nickie. Laura told me as much as she could about what she found at the Greenbelt."

Emily whirled away from the shelves. "She told *you* about the gorafrex?"

Carl's mouth twitched uncertainly until Nathan added, "She told me everything about it too. You're not breaking any confidences."

"Oh. Well, I…" The shop owner grabbed his empty teacup, raised it halfway to his lips, then realized it was empty and set it down again. "And that's why you're digging for iron?"

"The grounding element for a potion Nickie's

boyfriend is mostly done mixing up for us," Emily added and walked back toward the counter. "I hope."

"Your boyfriend?"

"That's not part of the Barton Creek problem," Nickie said. "We need to find the same iron that made these rings." She and Emily lifted their hands. "And the gorafrex's prison in the Greenbelt."

Carl puffed out a startled breath and blinked. "Why in the world would you need a piece of the *prison*?"

"Because that thing took our sister, Carl." Emily set her hands on the counter and leaned toward the man. "Because magic is about as useful as a box of tissues right now. Because the three of us are the only ones who can put the witch-killer back where it belongs before things get *worse*, and then we're the only ones who can make them better again."

Nathan took a step back from the counter and lifted his hands. "Not me. Three Hadstrom witches."

Carl stared at his customers, bit the inside of his bottom lip, shook a finger at the Hadstrom sisters, and turned away from the desk. "I might have something that can help. Not professional tools, by any means, but it's better than nothing."

"Sounds like a plan," Emily called after him as he retreated into the back room. Then she looked at Nickie with an unsure grimace. "I wasn't too hard on him, was I?"

"Actually, Em, that was the perfect amount of 'I'm serious and we need you.' I'm impressed."

"Thanks. I guess. I just...I don't wanna be going around strong-arming old dudes in antique stores, you know?"

"We were not planning on making a habit of it."

"And I'm not *that* old," Carl said as he stepped out of the back. "Well, I guess that depends on your definition of old." He dropped a heavy, hard-bound book onto the counter and laid a small, thin, delicate-looking silver hammer on the book's cover. "These, I think, will be your best bet."

Emily stared at the jeweler's hammer and popped her lips. "Got any dynamite?"

"Em…"

"This is a *toy*."

"Size isn't everything," Carl said. When Nathan snorted, the shop owner shot him a warning glance and lifted the tiny hammer, twirling it between his thumb and forefinger. "Historically—and I'm talking far before this ship was created, so it goes beyond the history of Earth and back to our original homes—the Kashgar, Huldus, and dwarves were the races best known for their skills with mining and the craftsmanship with which they turned their ore into salable goods."

"Okay." Emily frowned at the hammer. "That looks like a crafting hammer."

"It belonged to Thelonius Stoneguard, I've been told. I bought it off an elf who said his grandmother was once good friends with the miner. Of course, it's all hearsay, but I do know that this little hammer packs a much bigger punch than you might think."

"Does that claim come with a demonstration?"

"Are you kidding?" Carl set the hammer down beside the book and shook his head. "I tested it once out back and flattened a metal trashcan. You're just gonna have to take my word for that one."

Emily dipped her head in concession. "Sounds good to me."

"And I imagine it's a tool most similar to what may have been used to craft those rings. Which, I'm assuming, are also affected by this magical dry spell, correct?"

"For the most part, yeah." Nickie gestured toward the book. "And what's that?"

"Sold to me by a dwarf before he left Austin. I put a sticky note in there for you on the map of the Greenbelt, specifically. There might be others, but that's a good place to start."

"Great. We'll take 'em both."

"Okay." Carl leaned toward his register and punched in a few numbers. Then he stopped, closed his eyes, and waved them off. "I can't charge you for those."

"You should." Nickie nudged her sister with an elbow. "We can't promise that they'll be in one piece when we're finished."

Emily grabbed the tiny hammer and the book and pulled them across the counter. "I'm gonna choose to believe that wasn't supposed to be a direct insult." Then she grinned at Carl. "Thank you. We'll bring them back when we're done."

"That's fine. Just do what you have to do to bring Laura back. The rest can wait, can't it?"

Emily tucked the book under her arm and shrugged. "Not really. Magic's just getting worse. But it's the thought that counts." She shot him a wave and headed toward the door.

"Thanks, Carl," Nickie said. "I get why Laura always came to you first."

"Well, just don't tell her I gave those away for free." The man's eyes twinkled as he shot Nickie a conspiratorial wink. "Don't wanna leave the impression that I'm playing favorites here."

"You mean that you didn't charge us for something that'll help us save your favorite Hadstrom sister? Yeah, no problem. I can keep a secret." Nickie nodded and turned toward the door.

"Let's go!" Emily called.

"Thanks again," Nathan told Carl.

The shop owner pointed at him. "You do whatever you can to help them. I know there's not a lot of wiggle room as far as that creature's concerned, but still."

"I'm already on it. Nice to meet you."

"You too, Nathan." Carl leaned against his counter until his latest customers had disappeared through the front door. Then he sighed and reached for the teacup. "I hope that works."

This time, he got the cup to his mouth before remembering it was empty. With a snort, he walked into the back room again to pour himself more tea.

CHAPTER SIXTEEN

In the dim lighting of Brightwing Apothecary on Red River Street, Laura Hadstrom waited for the unmistakable sound of the front door slamming shut before she moved. "Okay, this is it."

Beside her, right where the gorafrex had left them both on the floor behind the desk, the apothecary owner stared at the round silver coin attached to the young witch's keyring. "Are you sure this will work?" Leonidas whispered, glancing nervously at the main door to his shop.

"No. I'm not sure." Laura pressed her dry lips together and gave her keyring a jingle. "But the gorafrex will be back soon. We know that much. And I have to try."

Leonidas rubbed his chin and nodded. "Of course. Just make it quick, okay? I can keep up this ruse of still being tied up like an animal about to be cooked over a spit, but I'm not sure I'll be able to come up with a good answer for why you're gone if that thing comes back before you do."

"I know. It won't take me long, I promise. I just need to get my sisters a message."

"Well, go ahead, then." The fairy leaned back against the underside of his desk and clenched his jaw in firm determination. "I'd help you, but…"

"You dislocated your shoulders for me," Laura said with a wink. "That was more than helpful." She took a deep breath, steeled herself, and pressed her thumb into the depressed thumbprint in the center of the Clubhouse charm on her keyring.

Leonidas stared at her hand. "Nothing's happening."

"Yeah, I know." Laura pressed her thumb against the coin even harder, but of course, pressure didn't have anything to do with whether or not magic decided to work in bits and pieces. "It's just a waiting game at this point. Until the gorafrex comes back, this is all I have."

"Okay." The fairy wiggled his jaw and cocked his head. "So, what is that thing supposed to do?"

"When we were kids, my sisters and I made this sort of secret room. We call it the Clubhouse, and we're the only ones who can get in."

"Is it safe?"

"Very." She looked up at his bright eyes, glinting at her from within the darkness under his desk. "My sister Nickie hears the gorafrex's drums. I know, it sounds weird. This drumbeat. It's like the thing's ancient call for witches and wizards. Lures them right to it if they're not careful. Which most magicals aren't anymore, because everyone forgot that that thing exists."

"It's a good reminder not to ignore history, isn't it?"

Laura snorted. "That's an understatement. But Nickie can't hear the gorafrex when she's in the Clubhouse, so if there's one place on this entire ship that's safe, it's this room we made. And technically, the Clubhouse isn't even—"

Laura Hadstrom popped out of existence behind the apothecary owner's desk. Leonidas started, sat up fully to peer into the darkness where the witch had just sat, and whispered, "Laura?"

A low, nervous chuckle escaped him, and he clapped both hands over his mouth to stifle it. "Just be quick about it."

Laura sat in the center of the Clubhouse and immediately took her thumb off the keyring charm. "Yes!" She laughed, jumped to her feet, and scanned the room, which hadn't changed in almost twenty years. "Okay, Laura. You're here to leave a message. Make it good."

She ducked under the origami jellyfish bobbing across the room, then reconsidered it and plucked it from the air. Then she hurried toward the kid-sized desk against the wall under the lava lamp and grabbed a red Sharpie from the can of markers, pens, and pencils. She wrote quickly, trying to fit everything she could onto one side of the flattened paper jellyfish. The paper bled with red ink, and the jellyfish fluttered under her hand. "Just hold on. I'm almost done."

A bright flash filled the Clubhouse, and she whirled around to look for the source. A strong pull tugged at her —not her shirt or her hand but at the core of her being. "No. No, not yet." She slammed her hand back down on the jellyfish and finished the last sentence of her message.

There was another bright flash, the walls of the Clubhouse wavered in and out, and she barely had time to drop the Sharpie and released the origami jellyfish before she was sucked back out of the Hadstrom sisters' secret hideout.

Leonidas gasped when she reappeared standing just beside his desk in Brightwing Emporium. "By the Aged Wing, girl. You scared the life out of me."

Laura dropped into a crouch, frowned at her keychain, and stuffed it back into her pocket. "Sorry. I didn't have much warning on that one, either."

"Did you get to leave your message?"

She settled back to sit against the wall behind the desk and nodded. "Barely. But I've never been pushed out of there before. The only way to get in or out is with that keyring charm. I should've had more time."

The fairy reached out to pat her gently on the knees. "Blame it all on magic, my dear. That's what I'm doing, and it might just be the only thing keeping me from tearing the rest of my hair out."

Laura eyed his balding head and let herself smile. "I do blame magic. But that part's my fault, too."

"I don't want to hear another self-shaming word out of your mouth, you understand? You've been kidnapped by that incredibly rude monster who staged a coup in my shop. And apparently, you're the only witch that thing could've brought here who has a chance of getting us out. Alive."

"Well, I just used the only thing I had up my sleeve. My sisters will have to do the rest."

Leonidas' eyes narrowed, and he leaned forward in a mixture of hope and conspiratorial eagerness. "You're certain they'll find your message and come for us?"

"Oh, yeah. I'm sure. I just helped point them in the right direction."

"Good. Now, before you so suddenly disappeared, you were saying something about this Clubhouse of yours."

"I was?"

"That it's the only room in the world safe from that creature. And then something about it not being…" Leonidas spread his arms.

"Right." Laura patted her back pocket to be doubly sure of her keys. "Technically, the Clubhouse isn't in the same dimension as the rest of this ship."

"It's not… How in the blazes did you manage to do that? As *children*?"

She let out a sigh and smiled. "I don't know, but we did, and that's what matters. My sisters will go there before they come looking for me. And *you*, of course. And they'll know what to do."

"I'll trust your judgment on that one." Leonidas rubbed his balding head. "The potions that creature's been putting together all night make for incredibly strong wards. I wouldn't mess with those unless I had a thorough knowledge of potionswork already under my belt."

"Well, that's where Emily comes in." Laura couldn't help but grin at the aged fairy. "I'm pretty sure she's even better than our—"

The front door to the long hallways leading into the apothecary's main room burst open and clicked shut a moment later. Hissing an aggravated breath through her teeth, Laura turned around on the floor and whispered at Leonidas over her shoulder, "Tie me up again. As fast as you can. It doesn't have to be perfect."

The fairy deftly did as he was told, both of them waiting for the silence to be shattered by the gorafrex in its latest human host barging into the room with them. He patted her wrist to let her know he was finished, then sat back under the desk and slipped his hands through the ropes that had bound his wrists behind him. "I pray that your sisters know what they're doing."

"Of course, they do," Laura whispered back. "Trust me, we're a lot safer in your shop than if that creature took us somewhere else."

"What do you mean?"

"Another part of the ship. In Austin. The gorafrex is trying to power a—"

The door to the main shop burst open next, and Laura sat back against the wall, pressing her lips together. The gorafrex's glowing silver eyes lit up in its human host's face as the door shut behind it. It took a deep breath through its host's nose and growled, "Get up."

Laura and Leonidas exchanged confused glances.

The gorafrex's inhuman voice poured from its host's mouth. "I hardly have the patience for what I've been forced to do without magic. I do not wish to repeat myself, witch."

Clenching her jaw, Laura pushed herself up against the wall until she stood. *Remember the ropes. It thinks you've been tied up this whole time.*

Slivers of light poured through the apothecary's drawn windows, and the gorafrex marched toward Laura and the desk at the back of the shop. "You too, fairy," it crooned. The false calm in that voice made Laura's skin crawl.

"I haven't done anything," Leonidas said, his voice rising in pitch. "You've taken over my shop and held me prisoner in it. Used up all my supplies. What do you want with—"

The gorafrex leapt behind the desk and peered under it at the aged fairy, snarling, "Do not make the mistake of thinking I am powerless without dependable magic. You are in no position to question me now. Get up."

Swallowing, Leonidas shuffled forward on his knees until he was out from under the desk. The gorafrex grabbed the fairy by the back of his shirt and hoisted him to his feet. "Your shop, your supplies, your word that what I've taken from your shelves is exactly what I said I need. I shall hold you to that." Those silver eyes flickered toward Laura and flashed again. "The fairy will keep *you* from trying anything stupid, witch."

"Oh, I hardly think there's anything *she* could do," Leonidas stammered. "Magic's off for everyone. What makes you so sure I can stop her from doing anything, even if she tried?"

The gorafrex jerked the old fairy out from behind the desk, then grabbed the back of Laura's shirt too and ushered them both into the center of the shop. "It's simple, isn't it?" The human host sneered at the magical prisoners in his tight grip. "This witch has been trying to stop me from the beginning. And she has failed. Many times. I assume you know it was she who released me in the first place?"

Leonidas' eyes bulged as he shot Laura a quick look of surprise.

"And it is she who will make me stronger." The gorafrex snarled again, then jostled Laura by the back of her shirt. "So if I do not get what I am owed, you will watch this fairy die in whatever way pleases me. Then I will take from you what I need."

Laura gritted her teeth and glared at those glowing silver eyes. "You won't get anything from me."

A grotesque chuckle escaped the witch-killer's human throat. "We shall see." It pulled Leonidas and Laura together, taking off the ropes binding them with one hand, and removed a vial from its host's back pocket. With a sharp, expectant breath, the gorafrex threw the vial on the ground at their feet. There was a flash of bright purple light, then all three of them disappeared, leaving behind Brightwing Emporium's mostly empty shelves and the smell of burning sugar.

CHAPTER SEVENTEEN

"Em, you're starting to make me nervous with that thing."

Emily wiggled the tiny dwarven hammer in her hand as she trudged along the footpath beside Barton Creek. "This? *This* is making you nervous?"

"If it's as strong as Carl said, then yeah." Nickie glanced back at Nathan, who was more concerned with scanning the Greenbelt for anyone else who happened to think a hike in the middle of the day in Austin's end-of-May heat was a great idea. "Seriously, though?"

"Yeah, okay." Emily stuck the hammer in her back pocket and wiped the sweat from her forehead. "Are we getting close?"

Nickie checked her phone for the hundredth time since they'd stepped out of her car. "Dad said it's just past the third swimming hole after the beach."

"We passed that five minutes ago."

"Right. Then there's a tree growing out of the creek."

"Huh." Emily stopped and placed her hands on her hips,

trying to catch her breath in the heat and humidity. The lashes on her forearm were burning again now that they were covered in sweat too. "Maybe we *should* go swimming."

"Later, Em." Nickie and Nathan both passed the youngest Hadstrom sister on the trail, and Emily rubbed her sweaty arm off on her shirt before trekking after them.

"I'm just sayin', if we're looking for a tree growing in the middle of the creek and get wet in the process, I'm not gonna complain about it."

The bugs droned, and a few birds flitted through the trees ahead of them. Emily watched their flight until they disappeared among the dogwood branches. "Hey, did you guys see any of the grackles before we left?"

"The ones hanging out at the side of your house?" Nathan asked, holding aside a few branches overgrown onto the footpath.

Emily stepped through the space he'd made, and he let the branches swing back into place. She glanced behind her, knowing it was crazy to think any of the plants out here could move on their own. *Just in the greenhouse. Nowhere else.*

"Yeah," she said and hurried after Nathan and her sister. "They still there?"

"I haven't made it a point to look, Em. Why?"

"Just curious. Wishful thinking, maybe. You know, like if the grackles start flying around and talking again, that would just be a sign that things aren't getting any worse, at least. And Laura was feeding them, so..."

"She was what?" Nathan looked back at her over his shoulder. "Grackles too?"

"She just can't help it," Nickie added, scanning the creek just off the footpath. "I mean, somebody's gotta help the messengers, right? When we get magic up and running again, those birds are gonna have a lot of work to do, ferrying all the new information back and forth."

Emily stopped with wide eyes. "You think they know what Laura did?"

"Yeah, Em. They fell on our house when magic started to sputter out. That wasn't a coincidence. *And* they know we're the only ones who can set things right again. So whatever messages they send when that happens will include that fact."

"Oh. I hope not."

"Why?"

Emily scrunched her nose and started down the path again. "Let's see. If all of Austin knows Hadstrom witches locked up a gorafrex—for the second time since this ship left on its original voyage—and that Hadstrom witches are responsible for putting magic back together before the city completely blows itself apart, we'll have magicals poppin' up all over the place, trying to shake our hands and thank us and tell us they couldn't be more grateful."

"That doesn't sound super-awful," Nickie said.

"Said the woman who has people screaming her name while she works. You might be rock-star material, Nickie, but there's a reason my job entails standing in the back of a restaurant where no one who's eating my food can see me."

Nathan wrong. "You have a hard time with accepting gratitude, Em?"

"What? No. I just don't wanna have to sit there and listen to everybody fall over themselves as they build us up into something we're not. That's not why we're doing this. It falls on us because we're Hadstroms, plain and simple. Maybe a little because Laura let that thing out—"

"By accident."

"I *know*. I was *going* to say that that part doesn't matter, though. Because this was our family's responsibility from the very beginning. It just doesn't feel right to be hailed for saving Austin's *magic* when that's what we were born to do."

Nickie turned around and grinned at her sister. "Wow, Em."

"What?"

"That might be the most mature opinion I've heard you give about anything."

Emily snorted. "You haven't heard me talk about how to fillet red snapper, have you?"

"Hold on." Nathan squinted and pointed through the overhanging live oak branches just off the path. "Does that look like a tree growing in the middle of the creek to you guys?"

Emily leaned past the edge of the path and nodded. "Yes. That's exactly what it looks like, Nate." She pounded his shoulder with her fist and took off, sliding down the hill toward the creek.

"Be careful," Nickie called after her. "We don't know what's over there."

"Yes, we do." Emily slid down the loose dirt until she reached the limestone boulders. A few bits crumbled under her shoes, but she managed to keep her footing long enough to hop down onto the pebbled riverbank. "The gorafrex's prison. Laura deactivated the wards the first time she came here. There's no witch-killer floating around the place it doesn't wanna be. And *maybe* we'll find some iron."

Shaking her head, Nickie headed after her sister, cradling the book Carl had given them under her arm. "Can you at least wait 'til we're all down there before you go splashing into the—"

Emily already had her shoes off and was sloshing through the creek's cool water. "Woah!" Her feet slipped on the moss-covered rocks of the creek bed, and she went down on one knee in the water with a wild laugh. "We need to come here more. You know, just for fun. Not to dig up ancient iron veins or to lock up the most dangerous magical stowaway on the entire ship." With a sigh, she splashed her face with water and gently rubbed the stinging slashes on her forearm. "This is the best thing ever."

Nickie set the dwarven book on a tree stump on the gravel beach, followed by her cell phone and keys, then kicked off her boots and rolled up the legs of her black skinny jeans. "Deal. Just don't go any closer to that tree without me, okay?"

Emily tossed her wet hair back and grinned. "Hurry up, then."

When Nickie waded into the creek, she couldn't help but laugh at how refreshing the cool water was in the heat, even if she was fully clothed. "You're totally right, though. This is amazing."

"I know."

The sisters turned around to wait for Nathan just as he finished pulling off his t-shirt and tossing it on the beach.

He slipped out of his sandals, stuck his phone next to Nickie's, and headed for the water. When he saw the Hadstrom sisters staring at him with wide eyes, he stopped. "What?" The man looked over his shoulder, but there was nothing there.

"You just…" Emily cleared her throat. "You took off your shirt and kept your pants on?"

Nickie elbowed her in the side.

"Uh…" He shot them a confused half-smile. "If I'd brought my swimsuit, it wouldn't be much different."

"Right." Nickie turned toward the willow growing from the creek bed and tugged on Emily's sleeve.

"It's just…" Emily laughed and shook her head. "You should come back here with Laura sometime, Nate. And don't tell her that we saw you with your shirt off before she did."

"Yeah, no problem. I'm pretty sure that won't come up in conversation." Nathan frowned after the youngest Hadstrom sister and followed them both through Barton Creek's cool water toward the huge willow in the center of it.

Nickie and Emily stopped in front of the cascading branches, which reached the water and floated in the light current.

"Wow. This is the spot."

"Yep." Nickie looked at her sister, then gazed at the top of the tree. "It's crazy to think that if Laura had just waited a day before coming here, Dad would've brought us instead."

"Yeah, and things would be a *lot* different right now."

"I'm gonna go ahead and say this, and it's more than just

playing devil's advocate." Nathan stopped on the other side of Emily and rubbed the back of his neck. "I'm glad she came here when she did."

"Because she needed your help with that rune," Nickie added.

"That's cute, Nate." Emily slapped the back of her hand against his arm and nodded. "Tell her *that*."

"When we get her back, yeah. I will."

Taking a deep breath, Emily reached out to brush aside the curtain of willow branches, then stepped into the shade of the tree that had guarded the gorafrex's prison for longer than they could comprehend.

"This is incredible," Nickie muttered when she stepped in.

"This is exactly the kind of place Laura would never be able to leave alone." Emily pointed at the bowl-shaped stone just in front of the willow's trunk. "And that's where the gorafrex got out. There's gotta be iron there, right? At least under that rock."

"Probably, yeah." There was only enough room for the Hadstrom sisters to crouch in front of the tree. Nathan stood within the curtain of willow branches, ankle-deep in the water. Nickie reached out with both hands to tug on the huge rock, then sighed and shook her head. "That thing's not gonna budge."

Emily wiggled her eyebrows and reached into her back pocket. "But we have a hammer."

"I don't know if *this* is the best place to use that, Em." Nickie studied the tree, the vines growing around its base, and the bowl-shaped stone with a huge crack running through the middle.

"What? This is the *best* place. Right at the source." Propping herself up on her elbows as she lay on her stomach in the soft grass, Emily tipped the delicate silver hammer back and forth. "Just have to hit the right spot."

Something thumped at the very top of the tree, shaking the cascading branches. The trio looked up at the thick curtain and the top of the willow's trunk, where a shadow passed over what little light spilled through. "Maybe it's just a bird," Emily muttered.

"That would be a really big bird." Nathan frowned, and the willow's draping branches shook and shivered again.

Two large, heavy somethings splashed into the creek outside the willow's hiding place, and the Hadstrom sisters scrambled back to their feet. Emily pocketed the hammer and grabbed her sister's hand. "Just in case."

"Right."

Nathan turned to slowly draw the branches aside. A few feet to his left, the branches were jerked open to reveal a furry, intelligent face. He staggered backward and slipped on the slick stones of the creek. He crashed into the water with a grunt and sat there staring at the haggard face watching them. "What—"

"It's okay," Nickie said quickly, then turned toward the wide, concerned eyes poking through the branches. "This is one of the Tree Folk, Nathan."

"The what now?"

The elf watching them drew the branches aside farther and blinked at the physics professor. "We are the Tree Folk," he croaked. Bright blue eyes—which had glistened with life and amusement the last time Nickie had seen him but were now dull and tired-looking—studied the professor for a few seconds from a face covered with light-brown fur. "We would have preferred to make your acquaintance under better circumstances, but, well, here we are. Please, we are waiting for you. And do not use that weapon here."

Emily blinked at the frail-looking member of the Tree Folk and muttered, "I put it away."

The creature nodded and withdrew, dropping the branches and leaving Nickie and Emily wondering what could have made the Tree Folk come to them now.

Nathan wondered if he'd fallen hard enough into the creek to start seeing things.

CHAPTER EIGHTEEN

When Nathan and the Hadstrom sisters emerged from the cover of the willow's branches again, they found the Tree Folk waiting for them. The one who'd spoken to them crouched beside the tree stump on the beach, thumbing through the dwarven book from Hopkins Antiques. Two others stood beside the limestone boulders, gazing around Barton Creek with concerned eyes. At least a dozen others watched from the overhanging branches of the dogwoods and live oaks as the trio waded across the creek again.

"Something's wrong," Nickie muttered before she and her sister reached the bank.

"Yeah, they look sick. Is that even possible?"

"We're about to find out."

The elf squatting beside the tree stump, who was dressed in frayed pants the color of pine needles and nothing else over his chest covered in the same light-brown fur as his face, looked up from the book. When

Nickie and Emily approached, instead of standing, the elf sat back on the gravel and let out a sigh.

Emily looked at the Tree Folk watching them from the trees along the footpath and waved. "Hey, everybody. Fancy seeing you again, especially since Nickie didn't call you out of hiding with her guitar skills this time."

"No." The elf in front of them shook his head. "We came of our own choosing today. To warn you."

"We've met before, haven't we?" Nickie said softly, coming to sit in front of the only member of the Tree Folk who seemed strong enough to speak to them—barely. He nodded in response and held her gaze while Emily and Nathan moved up the beach to join them.

In the darkness beneath the willow, it had been hard to tell, but now it was unmistakable. The Tree Folk—all of them—were not the healthy, laughing, playful creatures who'd told the Hadstrom sisters about the gorafrex's only weakness two weeks ago. Every face was haggard and thin, every pair of eyes lacking the shine of ageless intelligence. Their fur was matted in most places, thinning in others, and their faces had lost their fullness where clumps had fallen out. The Tree Folk had always been lithe and thin, having spent centuries on this ship living within the trees. Now, they looked starved.

"You said you came to warn us," Emily said, glancing at the two Tree Folk standing in front of the boulders. "We already know the gorafrex has our sister Laura. We know it's trying something with potions. Wards, most likely. And we know that magic keeps breaking apart the longer it takes us to find her and put that thing back in its prison."

She gestured toward the willow, and the elf sitting in front of them nodded.

"Yes. We all feel what is happening now."

"I thought you weren't allowed to get involved?" Nickie held the creature's gaze, hoping he remembered when he'd come to her in secret—to warn her of her childhood lullaby and the power it held to call the gorafrex to her.

"Things have changed, Nickie Hadstrom." He looked over his shoulder at the rest of his people settled in the trees behind him. He blinked slowly. "We did not foresee the events that would lead to magic undoing itself here in our home. The gorafrex has had much time to ponder how far it is willing to go to reach its aims. We cannot endure much longer if that creature is not stopped. Soon."

"It's making you sick, isn't it?" Emily glanced at all the frail, haggard-looking bodies.

"We are as connected to the ship's magic as any other magical who uses it," the elf replied. "For now, the danger has not spread farther than this place you call Austin, Texas. We cannot say if that will last, or for how much longer."

"You could leave, though, right?" Emily gestured behind her toward the miles of open woodland of the Greenbelt and beyond. "If magic still works outside of Austin, it would be safe for you there. And you wouldn't have to—"

"We would leave our home to its fate just as readily as you would," the elf told her. "Are you willing to step away from your home, your duty here, just to reclaim magic elsewhere while you still can?"

The youngest Hadstrom sister blinked, searched the faces in the trees, and shook her head. "Not a chance."

"Then you understand us and why we all agreed to find you today."

Nickie swallowed and nodded. "I'm so sorry this is happening to you and your people. We're doing everything we can as fast as we can. We hit a setback when the gorafrex took Laura, though."

"Yes. You cannot fulfill your duty without a third Hadstrom witch." The elf nodded slowly. "But we did not come to warn you of what might happen if you do not. This, we think, you already know." The sisters nodded. "That hammer in your pocket."

"Yeah." Emily patted her pocket again to be sure it was still there. "Just picked it up from a friend."

"And we almost were too late to keep you from making another grave mistake. Do not use this gift from a friend on the broken door." The Tree Folk's spokesperson gestured toward the willow in the creek. "Or it will not close again once the prisoner has returned."

"Oh, boy." Emily closed her eyes. "I almost blew up the prison, huh?"

"But you did not." The elf set a hand on the tree stump and used it to push himself up on one knee. "This is a useful tome you've brought with you. There is a—" He winced when he tried to stand and nearly toppled over.

"Careful." Nickie stood and offered him a hand, but he waved her off.

It took a few seconds for the elf to regain his balance, but he did and stood to his full height. "This book of yours has the knowledge that will help you find the grounding source you seek. That is the reason you are here, correct?"

"For the iron, yeah." Emily looked up at him and lifted

her hand to show him her copper legacy ring. "The same that made our rings."

"And that prison, yes. This is where you must go. There is a cavern in this place, though that is not the exact word. A place as old as that prison. You will find what you need there, and not beneath the branches of that tree."

"Can you give us more direction than that?"

The elf shook his head, grimacing again at the pain of some unseen injury. A small tuft of fur released itself from his arm and fluttered to the graveled beach. He didn't seem to notice. "We do not have much knowledge of what lies below the surface. Our hearts and our wisdom belong to the trees." Above him, the Tree Folk listening in the branches nodded, mumbling their agreement. Even that movement was lethargic and seemed to leave them in even more discomfort.

"Any helpful hints about where to find it?" Emily pushed herself to her feet and nodded at the book on the tree stump. "Is it in the book?"

"No. But your companion has the knowledge inside him." The elf lifted a shaking hand and pointed at Nathan. "It is this he must access to lead you to where you need to go."

"Me?" Nathan gestured to himself and frowned at the Hadstrom sisters. "I don't know anything about a cavern connected to a prison for the gorafrex. Sorry."

"We knew your ancestors." A female voice echoed toward them from the branches, though the Tree Folk member who'd spoken remained hidden. "Proud Kashgar, all of them. Skilled craftsmen. Sworn to protect this ship, its cargo, and all its passengers. *That* is their legacy.

Remember that and do not trouble yourself with the rest of it."

Nathan's eyes narrowed as he searched the branches for the speaker. "Noted."

"We have already stayed too long," the elf added. "It is time for us to rest, and for you to do what you must so we might reclaim our strength. We hope our next meeting is under much better circumstances than these." He turned and headed up the beach toward his two brethren standing beside the boulders.

"Wait." Nickie went after him, but the creature didn't respond until she said, "I think I can help you."

The elf looked at her over the matted fur on his shoulder. "You will once the creature is imprisoned and magic is restored."

"No, I mean right now. Just a little, and it probably won't last as long as either of us wants it to, but I want to try. Please."

The monkey-like creature glanced up at his people in the trees, but none of them moved or gave any reply. "What do you have for us?"

"A song."

The elf's smile was slow and sad and made him look every bit as old as the centuries his people had spent on this ship. "We enjoyed your music very much, Nickie Hadstrom. But magic is not what it should be."

"My music is, though." Nickie took another step toward him and nodded. "It's just a different kind of magic. Like potions."

"That's *right*." Emily grinned and pointed at her sister. "She sang a gorlek out of burning us to a crisp. And this morning, one song from Nickie sorted all the books in the library's restricted section back into their…well, into piles, at least. By subject matter." Nickie gave her a warning glance, and Emily spread her arms. "It's true."

"Do you have a song for healing a people suffering from the broken source that feeds them?" His eyes were wide now, almost hopeful. Above them, the Tree Folk whispered to each other. The branches rustled for a few seconds, then fell still. A dozen pairs of eyes blinked down at Nickie Hadstrom on the beach beside Barton Creek, all of them waiting for the relief a different kind of magic might provide them.

"I'm pretty sure I do," Nickie said. "Will you let me try?"

With a deep breath, the elf bowed his head and closed his eyes. "It would be our pleasure."

When Nickie glanced at her sister, Emily gave her a reassuring nod and whispered, "Time for a different kind of healing, I think."

Nickie reached out to take her sister's hand. "Just in case." The legacy rings on both Hadstrom sisters' thumbs flashed, the light muted by the bright sun in a clear sky over the Greenbelt, and Austin's new Queen of Blues started to sing.

CHAPTER NINETEEN

"Okay, you should put that on your list of top five best performances ever." Emily wiped the sweat off her forehead and stared at now-empty branches of the trees reaching over the beach by the creek.

"Thanks, Em."

"No, I'm serious. That was amazing, and you didn't even need a guitar for that one. Serious skills."

Nathan stooped to pick up the dwarven book from the tree stump, tucked it under his arm, and glanced up at the trees too. "Coming from someone who's never seen you live before, I'm gonna have to agree with Emily on that one."

"What?" Emily blinked at him. "You've never heard her play?"

"Well, just once." Nathan nodded at Nickie and smiled. "Not really playing, I guess. But it was awesome."

Nickie peeled her hair away from her sweaty face and neck. "I hope it was enough."

"It had to be. They were *laughing* when they disappeared through the trees, Nickie, and it wasn't *at* you."

"They did seem to liven up, huh?"

Emily chuckled as she pulled her shoes and socks back on. "You gave them a musical anesthetic."

Nathan stuck his thumb out toward Emily and cocked his head. "She's killing it with the analogies today."

"Thanks, Nate."

Nickie stepped back into her boots, frowning at the tooth marks in the toe of the left one. "Wish I knew how long it'll last for them, though. It clearly took a lot out of them to come find us here."

"It was an excellent way to thank them. Plus, your ring was helping you out with healing spells when magic followed the rules. I think your music figured out how to boost that part." Emily stood and reached for the tiny hammer in her back pocket. "And I needed a good reminder to think before I hammer."

"Which leads us right back to why we're here." Nickie looked at Nathan, who'd put his shirt and shoes back on faster than either of the Hadstrom sisters. "Any idea how you're supposed to access your Kashgar roots?"

"Sort of. Maybe." He let out a wry chuckle and stared into the trees again. "This might sound nuts, so stop me if it's just too far outside the realm of possibility, okay?"

"Hey, Nickie just healed the Tree Folk with a solo acoustic performance. I'm carrying around a tiny hammer that apparently would've destroyed an entire prison, so the realm of possibility isn't what we're going for right now."

"Touché." Nathan rubbed his chin and took a deep breath. "I'm gonna lie down and listen to the ground."

"Oh." Emily fought back a laugh, then nodded vigorously. "Not what I expected you to say, but do what you gotta do."

"Yep." Nathan headed toward the wall of limestone boulders close to the footpath at the top of the rise and stopped beneath the overhanging branches. The Hadstrom sisters followed him and sat a few feet away as Nathan lowered himself to the ground and stretched out on his back, his arms folded behind his head. "You don't have to be quiet. Just pretend we don't have anything else to do right now."

"That's gonna be hard," Nickie said, leaning back against one of the boulders.

"I know."

They sat there next to Nathan for at least five minutes before Emily leaned toward her sister and whispered, "I think he fell asleep."

Nickie eyed the physics professor, who hadn't moved an inch since he'd sprawled out, and shrugged. "We'll give him another five minutes."

"I hope Laura has another five minutes."

"Hey, we're all trying to do this as fast as we can, Em. Including Nathan."

Emily sighed and plucked a handful of grass from the ground beside her. "That's not what I meant. I know we have to do this right, and we need that grounding iron for this next potion. I just *really* don't like sitting around and waiting."

Nickie snorted. "You remember what Grandma Eloise used to say about waiting?"

Wobbling her head like their grandmother and rolling her eyes, Emily imitated Greg Hadstrom's mother to perfection. "Anything worth your time is worth waiting for, girls. Now get your grubby little hands out of that cookie jar and go play outside. I'll call you when dinner's ready."

"That was really good."

"Grandma Eloise's sayings left a pretty big impression on me."

Nickie chuckled. "I can tell."

"And I think I do the exact opposite now. How weird is that?"

"You just don't like being told what to do, Em. That's a family trait too."

Emily shrugged. "So is being the best at what we do, right?"

The sisters fell into silence then, surrounded by the babble of the shallow creek beside them and the buzzing drone of the cicadas in the woods.

"Has it been five minutes yet?"

Nickie reached into her back pocket for her phone. "Nope. We have another—"

Nathan took a huge, sudden breath, and the Hadstrom sisters jolted in surprise. He pushed himself up and blinked a few times, then turned to shoot Emily and Nickie a knowing smile. "I found it."

"You *found* it?" Emily asked.

"The cavern? Yeah." He pushed himself to his feet, tucked the book under his arm, and nodded upriver. "We were heading in the right direction."

"Then we just keep going. Lead the way, O part-Kashgar guide."

Nathan shot her a playful frown and moved through the shade beneath the trees. The Hadstrom sisters followed him upriver, all of them searching the woods for anything that looked remotely like a cave or a cavern or something that wasn't what it seemed.

They'd gone about a mile when Nathan stopped and cocked his head. "We're close."

"What are we looking for?" Emily turned in a slow circle. "Runes carved into a giant rock? A staircase under a tree? Anything?"

"I honestly have no idea what it looks like," Nathan muttered, stepping over fallen branches and heading toward the creek again. "I'm going by feel alone. I think we need to be on the other side of the creek."

"Excellent. Lead on."

They didn't bother to take off their shoes this time, which wouldn't have made a difference as they stepped over a natural pathway of large flat stones jutting from the water. A few yards farther upriver, the creek bed lifted in a shallow waterfall flowing toward them, the sound barely rising above the buzzing insects. Nickie brought up the rear across the creek, and the Hadstrom sisters stood there, waiting for Nathan to figure out their next move.

"Okay. This way." He ducked beneath the low-hanging live oak branches. The woods grew even thicker here, providing a lot more shade and a lot less breeze to blow away the humidity.

Emily's shoes squelched in a puddle of thick mud and

she shook off her shoe, trying to wipe the mess off on the grass. "Have you always been able to *feel* where you're going?"

"Mostly. I had to figure that part out on my own, though. Not a lot of people in the family willing to talk in-depth about the Kashgar side. Pretty sure we've missed out on a lot of what we can do that way, but I've tried to learn what I can." The ground dipped below them until they stood in a depression of ground just beside the waterfall. The water rushed around them, and Nathan turned toward the side of the hill and the river to run his hand along the moss-covered rocks. "There is something here."

"Anything we can do to help?" Nickie asked, scanning the normal-looking hillside.

Nathan shrugged and kept drawing his hand over the earth in front of him.

"Okay, how 'bout this?" Emily withdrew the tiny silver hammer from her pocket and pointed it at the wall. "Now do I get to use this thing?"

"Nope." Nickie lowered her sister's arm and pointed at Nathan. "He'll figure it out."

"Almost there, guys." He cocked his head and closed his eyes, then stopped trailing his hand over the rock wall. "*Et apertum est* Kashgar, Nathan Reynolds."

The ground trembled beneath them and started to sink. Smaller rocks and fallen leaves and the grass growing in the depression in the earth tumbled toward each other, and Nickie grabbed Emily's wrist to pull her back up the rise. On the other side of the sinkhole, Nathan climbed toward the trees upriver and steadied himself against the rock wall.

Finally, when the ground stopped moving, all three of them stared at what the professor had found and opened for them.

"Just one more question," Emily muttered. "Did you know you were looking for a hidden staircase built into the side of a waterfall?"

Nathan looked up at her and raised his eyebrows. "I would *really* love to be able to take credit for that."

Nickie stepped past her sister and headed for the top of the stairs. "You get all the credit, Nathan. Anybody else think all of our ancestors were down here together at one point?"

Emily peered into the dark hole at the bottom of the stairs and hummed in thought. "How much you wanna bet everything down there is a lot less cutting-edge than when our ancestors were here?"

"It's not a bet if the other person agrees with you, Em." Nickie grinned at her sister and nodded into the darkness. "You ready?"

"Always." Emily stepped down onto the first step and let out a sharp laugh. "Laura's gonna be really miffed about missing out on this one."

"Don't worry," Nathan said. "When everything's back to normal again, I'll bring her here too."

"And that'll just make you her favorite person ever." Emily's voice echoed from the darkness as she disappeared below the rock wall.

Nickie stepped down behind her sister, and Nathan just shrugged. "Yeah, I think I can live with that."

CHAPTER TWENTY

The stairs were damp with spray from the creek's small waterfall and so many decomposing leaves and vegetation that had been part of the forest floor for who knew how long. When they reached the bottom of the stairs, the chamber there wasn't much drier but was much darker than the thick woods above them.

"Can you guys see anything?" Emily's voice echoed in a room that sounded way too big.

"Nope," Nickie replied.

"I can see enough." Nathan made his way past Nickie's dark outline and stopped between the Hadstrom sisters.

"Your Kashgar side is in full swing right now, huh?" Emily chuckled. "You *can* see in the dark, right?"

"It's more like my eyes adjust extra quickly in darker-than-normal places." The physics professor stared at the chamber, the control panels that had long since fallen into disrepair, the viewing screen beneath the waterfall, and the bed of Barton Creek. "This is definitely where we wanna be right now."

"Okay, I need a light."

"Just follow my voice, Nickie." Smirking, Emily turned around and waved her hands through the air, searching for her sister. "Marco…"

Nickie stepped right into Emily's outstretched hands, ducking away from the wiggling fingers. "Ow. Put your hands away, Em. You almost poked my eyes out."

"But you found me."

A pale yellow glow rose behind Emily, and the sisters spun to see Nathan's silhouette backlit by a dim yellow bubble blooming in his hand. Then the bubble's light sputtered, the sphere of his spell popped with a wet burst, and the darkness returned.

"This is so frustrating," he muttered.

"I was about to get excited about magic opening a window for real spells right now." Emily sighed, found Nickie's shoulder, and squeezed it. "Ready to try a jumpstart?"

"Let's do it."

Both legacy rings flashed on the sisters' thumbs. A burst of blazing white light exploded from the rings and ballooned out to fill the entire chamber. The Hadstrom witches and Nathan ducked away from the glare, shielding their eyes until the double-witch-powered spell settled into an orb of light on the chamber's ceiling that seemed more fluorescent than naturally glowing.

"Well, at least we can see." Emily blinked rapidly, trying to clear the image of Nathan's silhouetted back burned into her retinas. "So, where are we? Woah!"

Nathan glanced at them, then gestured toward the opposite wall with the non-functioning control panels and the swivel chairs and the symbols etched into metal and stone. "If we're comparing the prison our ancestors built for the gorafrex to something on the surface," he said, blinking and turning in a slow circle, "this would be a watchtower."

"This is incredible." Nickie tossed her hair out of her eyes and gazed at the massive blank wall at the far end of the chamber. "That looks like a projection screen. Or a window, maybe?"

"Probably both," Nathan replied.

"So witches and Kashgars and Huldus and Velikan Engineers built this thing just after the ship launched, huh?" Emily stepped away from her sister and approached the rows of dead control panels. Her foot knocked against something that filled the chamber with an echoing tinny clang, and she glanced down to see what looked like a metal lunchbox, complete with rusted locks, dented sides, and a frayed handle. "And then they took shifts manning the place to watch how the heck a bodiless gorafrex would spend its time in centuries of solitary."

"That's just depressing," Nickie muttered.

"And probably accurate." Nathan walked toward the screen on the far wall. "I wonder how long it's been since anyone was down here?"

"Long enough for the rest of Austin to forget."

"No," Emily corrected. "The Tree Folk knew about it, just not how to find it. I'm sure Rutilda remembers, somewhere behind all those cobwebs in her giant head."

"Who?"

The youngest Hadstrom sister shrugged. "The Velikan Engineer who told Laura about the energy cores. The one who went stomping around the city and crushing everything in her path before the Huldus—" She swallowed and shook her head.

"Wiped John's memory," Nathan finished for her. "I get it."

"Yeah, I was kinda trying to stop before those words could come out, but thanks for the moral support."

"We found it." Nickie's boots whispered across the stone floor covered in centuries of dust. "And the grounding element is supposed to be here."

"The original iron." Emily nodded. "Or whatever."

"This is just a guess," Nathan said, pointing at a series of symbols carved a few inches into the wall beside the screen, "but I'm thinking that's probably what 'Isolation Vein' means."

Nickie scoffed. "Uh, yeah. That sounds like it would fit. Did you just pull that out of thin air?"

"What? No." The part-Kashgar went to the runes and made an L beside them with his arms. "It's carved into the wall."

"There's *something* carved into the wall." Emily squinted at the symbols she couldn't read and stepped toward him. "Looks like someone had fun with a… Well, I'm guessing the people who built this place had a lot more to work with than a hammer and chisel."

"You guys can't read this?"

"Nope."

"Not even a little?"

Nathan ruffled his dark hair, the light violet hue of his eyes still glowing under the fluorescent brightness of the

Hadstrom sisters' illumination orb. "That's a new one for me."

"Looks like the part-Kashgar can read full-Kashgar symbols." Emily grinned at him. "I'm glad you forced yourself onto this mission with us, Nate."

He chuckled and ran a hand over the deep grooves in the stone. "Me too. I think."

"The question now is whether you can open that thing," Nickie said. "If it even opens."

"I'm sure it was supposed to." The physics professor stepped away from the symbols, studied them intently for a few more seconds, then pressed both hands against the wall and bowed his head.

Nothing happened.

"Okay." His chest rose and fell with a huge sigh. "You think you guys could maybe lend a hand over here."

"Totally."

"Yeah, we got you."

The Hadstrom sisters quickly crossed the chamber, and each set a hand on one of Nathan's shoulders. Smirking, Nickie put her hand on the back of Emily's neck. Her sister flinched before letting out a subdued chuckle. "All we need now is to start chanting, and this would probably qualify as making our own cult."

Nickie snorted and shook her head.

"Just think about opening it, yeah?" Nathan smiled with his eyes still closed and cocked his head.

"Got it."

"Yep."

The next second, both legacy rings flashed on the sisters'

thumbs. No spells came from the Hadstrom witches this time, but the connection they made with magic was enough to fuel the spell Nathan's Kashgar and Peabrain sides wanted to cast.

A warm yellow glow bloomed on his shoulders beneath the sisters' hands, coursing down his arms and into his fingers before seeping into the wall. The spell's light poured into the inches-deep grooves of the Kashgar runes until the symbols glowed almost as bright as the orb hovering just below the ceiling.

Nathan took a quick, shuddering breath and pulled his hands away. "That was wild."

"You mean the part about casting a spell without magic working for anyone else? Or that you can light up holes dug into a wall?" Emily let out a wry chuckle, and they all stepped back from the stone.

"I mean the part about being able to feel magic from two different witches shooting through my body." A chill raced up Nathan's back, and he shook it out of his shoulders and neck. "That's another first for me."

"Don't make a big deal out of it." Emily stared at the glowing runes pulsing with yellow light, which was getting brighter by the second. "Right now, the Hadstrom witch jumper cables, potions, and Nickie's music are the only things working right now."

"Still crazy to be a part of," Nathan muttered.

Nickie wrinkled her nose at the pulsing runes and frowned. "We cast your spell, Nathan. Was it supposed to *do* something, or—"

The stone floor trembled beneath them, followed by a groaning rumble as the entire chamber shuddered. The trio stepped farther away from the wall, and the glowing runes blinked bright yellow. Sheets of ancient dust and pebbles and dirt from the surface rained down around them. With a deafening crack, a thick fissure broke the wall in front of them, cutting through the runes from the ceiling down to the floor, and the yellow light of their combined spell winked out.

"Uh-oh." Emily turned around and glanced back at the open staircase, where chunks of dirt and piles of sodden, moldy leaves tumbled into the chamber's entrance. "Maybe we shouldn't just be standing here waiting for something to happen."

"It's already happening, Em. Look." Nickie pointed at the giant crack running down the wall through the runes, and the chamber walls started to move.

CHAPTER TWENTY-ONE

"Nathan. You're the part-Kashgar here in our blind search party." Emily stumbled sideways as the ground bucked beneath her. The centuries-old lunchbox skidded across the chamber with another tinny echo. "Can you say with a hundred percent certainty that we didn't just break this place?"

"Maybe ninety-five-percent." Nathan crouched and squared his footing as the walls covered in Kashgar runes moved apart from each other.

Emily shrugged. "I guess that's still pretty sure."

One of the doors sliding back into the chamber wall—they were definitely doors, separated by the crack through the runes—lodged on an errant hunk of stone and rumbled. It shuddered, cracked again, and the whole bottom half of the moving wall crumbled away. The rubble spilled into the hidden room beyond the doors, and then all the trembling stopped.

For a few seconds, Nathan and the Hadstrom sisters stood there in silence, staring into the thick darkness of the passage they'd just opened with the combined magic of three people. A few smaller chunks of rock wiggled free from the chamber ceiling and thumped into Emily's head.

"Ow!" She kicked the rocks aside, ducking and rubbing her head as she shot a scathing glance at the ancient ceiling. "That wasn't necessary."

"Get the light in there." Nickie grabbed her sister's arm and waved at the orb. When her ring flashed, the illumination orb dropped from the ceiling and barreled into the dark room through the crumbled doors. It smacked against the far wall, blinking and sputtering furiously, then settled into its bright fluorescence again and bobbed against the next chamber's lower ceiling. "Wow."

Emily pried her sister's firm grip from her arm and rubbed the soreness there. "We did it. We found the grounding element."

"Em, I'm pretty sure we found the place where *all* this happened." Nickie gestured around the room, which was covered in a lot less dust than the main chamber after having been sealed off for thousands of years. "Building the prison. Making the rings. Locking up the gorafrex. All of it."

"Huh. Doesn't look like an Engineer could fit inside."

"The Engineers worked a lot farther underground, didn't they?" Nathan joined the sisters as they stepped cautiously over the crumbled stone and through the split doors.

"Yeah. They wouldn't have had to come up here for the rings. Or to watch the gorafrex on that screen." Nickie turned to her sister. "We've seen one of those before. In one of the energy core chambers."

"I remember that now." Emily rubbed her hands together. "Looked like a window, but there wasn't anything on the other side. Wait, you think the Engineers were watching that thing in its prison too?"

"Probably while they built the escape pod and set up all the energy cores, yeah."

"And it all stemmed from this." Nathan crossed the smaller room and pointed at the bright silver line of metal two feet thick cutting through the center of the room. "The runes said, 'Isolation Vein,' making this a literal vein of pure iron, right?"

"Your guess is as good as mine." Emily stepped to the thick silver line on the stone floor, studying it. "It looks like iron to me."

"I thought it was supposed to be darker."

"Not when it's stripped of all the extra stuff." Nickie nodded at the physics professor. "That's as far as our knowledge of pure iron goes. But you've seen the weapons Laura's ring made us, right?"

Emily grinned and squatted in front of the iron vein. "Same bright silver and everything."

"Huh." Nathan folded his arms and stared at the floor. "I'm gonna defer to you guys on this one."

"I think you've earned it." Nickie patted him on the shoulder. "I don't know if we would've found this without you."

"And we'll make sure Laura hears that part." Emily winked at him, then pulled the tiny silver hammer from Hopkins Antiques out of her back pocket. "I'm so ready to use this thing."

Nickie took a tentative step toward her sister. "Em,

maybe we should look this thing over a little bit more just to—"

"Stop." Emily reached toward her sister's root-chewed boot, then lifted the tiny silver tool and wiggled her eyebrows. "Hammer time."

Nathan barked a laugh. Nickie tried to fight back her chuckle and finally just shook her head. "You've been sitting on that one since you took it off Carl's counter."

"Duh." Emily shifted in her squat for better momentum. "I'm gonna knock a piece of pure iron out of this Isolation Vein. Then we're gonna drop it in a potion and get our sister back."

"Want a count?" Nickie muttered with a smirk.

"That'd be pretty cool."

"Gently, Em."

"Come on. Give me a little credit here."

"One…two…*three*."

Emily struck the vein of iron on the floor with the hammer. A piercing, high-pitched ring of metal on metal filled the small chamber, followed by a streak of purple that crackled like lightning across the iron until it disappeared. Nothing else.

"Seriously?" The youngest Hadstrom sister stared at the head of the tiny silver hammer and scowled. "Carl's so full of it. Packs a punch. Yeah, right."

"This place has been empty for a long time," Nickie said. "Maybe it just needs a little time to respond."

"Maybe. Maybe not." Without any warning, Emily threw her arm back and brought the silver hammer crashing down onto the iron vein. A thunderous report rang through the air, and the entire line of iron running through the chamber lit up with violent purple light. The hammer sailed from Emily's hand, spinning end over end until it struck the far wall of the inner chamber. It didn't stop there.

Crash after crash echoed as the dwarven jeweler's hammer knocked through who knew how many miles of bedrock beneath Barton Creek. Finally, though, the rolling thunder of the tiny tool's destruction faded into silence.

Emily stared at the gaping hole the hammer had left in the wall. Another sheet of crumbled rock and dust fell in front of the bashed-in stone, and she flinched. "From here on out, I'm gonna take everything that man says as gospel."

"Another lesson learned, huh?"

The youngest Hadstrom witch turned slowly to look at Nickie and shot her sister a sheepish smile. "I hope you're not making a list."

"Is Carl the kind of man who would be upset about losing a dwarven artifact he let us borrow? For free?"

Neither of the sisters looked at Nathan. Nickie smacked her lips. "Probably not."

"We'll just tell him it was a casualty of saving magic and Austin and probably the entire ship after we put the gorafrex away. Right here." Emily pressed her hand to the stone floor and shivered. "That's trippy."

"And at least we can tell him the hammer did help us." Nickie squatted beside her sister, and they studied the glowing purple fragments within the vein of iron. "Looks like you broke it up, Em. Or at least cracked it enough that we can try to get out a decent-sized piece."

Together, the sisters ran their hands along the fractured

iron ore, feeling it for divots or larger cracks. "Man, what I wouldn't give for a couple of teezlers right now."

Nickie chuckled. "They'd get the job done without even trying."

"A couple of teezlers." Nathan shot them a playful frown. "You know what those are, right?"

"Of course, we do." Emily picked at a thicker crack in the iron but gave up and moved on when it wouldn't budge. "We have a whole nest of them in the basement. Feels like just yesterday that that little stowaway bashed in our first energy core under the Thinkery."

"Probably 'cause it was just two weeks ago," Nickie added.

"Or that."

Nathan sighed. "I thought I'd gotten to know you guys pretty well since I met Laura."

Emily grinned up at him. "And now you think you were wrong?"

"Not really. Just that there's a lot more to the three of you than I expected."

"I'll take *that* as a compliment, professor." Nickie pointed at him without looking up from the wide crack in the iron she was currently trying to wedge her fingers into.

"Take it however you want." Nathan let out a chuckle of disbelief. "I'm still trying to figure it out."

"Just roll with it, Nate. The Hadstrom sisters aren't a nice little physics equation you can just solve and—oh! Nickie, right here." Emily wiggled the fragment of iron where she'd cracked it open. It was about the size of a quarter and still wedged deeply into the rest of the ore. "We need to get this out."

"How much do we need?"

"Not nearly this much, but I forgot to bring my iron grater and the little collection bottle for shavings."

Nickie stared at her. "You don't have those things."

"No. I was banking on the tiny hammer."

Nickie sat back on her heels and pointed at the wobbling fragment of iron. "Okay. I have an idea."

Another crash rumbled toward them from much deeper in the earth, spilling through the hole the dwarven hammer had made in the chamber. Nathan dropped into a squat on the other side of the iron vein and caught the sisters' gazes with wide eyes. "Ideas are good as long as you guys are quick about it. I don't think we have a lot of time left in here."

"Like before the doors slide shut again and lock us in here forever?" Emily asked. "Or..."

The ground trembled again beneath them, followed by the very clear sounds of crashing stone and rushing water.

"Like before the holes that hammer made cave in and we get crushed under all of it." Nathan up at the ceiling, which now dripped water in a few places. Most of the earth above them was coated in a thin layer of creek. "We're right under the creek and the waterfall and there is a serious lack of structural integrity."

"You and Laura really are perfect for each other, you know that?"

"Em!"

"Right."

Nickie set a hand on her sister's knee and nodded. "Just keep wiggling that thing. Got it?"

"Yep. And your plan?"

"It's not a plan, just an idea."

The earth's next groan sounded a lot closer, and a lot more dust and dirt spilled down on them from the ceiling.

"It's gotta be a quick idea," Nathan warned.

"I'm getting there." Nickie closed her eyes, took a deep breath, and started to sing.

"Um, Nickie?" Emily flicked her gaze toward Nathan, who had no idea what he was hearing. "Hey, you can't sing that right now. Dad's lullaby is for the *gorafrex*, remember? You wanna bring that thing running to this secret room and crush us down here even faster?"

Nickie stopped abruptly and whispered, "It's *different*, Em. I know what I'm doing."

"Do you? Because it sounds a lot like you're singing the one song you're not supposed to sing until we're ready to take that thing down."

Opening her eyes, Nickie shot her sister a burning glare. Emily couldn't help but turn away from the look that had gotten her into more fights with her slightly older sister than she cared to remember as an adult. "Yeah, okay."

Nathan cleared his throat. "You sure—"

Nickie started singing again, and Emily looked at him with wide eyes. "That was her 'I'll hide all your best knives if you don't do what I say right now' face. She's good."

When Nickie flicked her sister's arm, Emily returned her attention to the loose piece of iron. "This must be what a kid's dentist feels like. There's gotta be a better way to just— Woah."

The song all the Hadstrom sisters knew so well—the lullaby Greg Hadstrom had sung to them since before they were born—had morphed and shifted into something completely different. The tune was the same, the notes of the melody in all the right places, but this song had three voices rising and falling one on top of one another in a twisted chord of sound.

The shard of iron in Emily's fingers vibrated in the rhythm of the notes of Nickie's lullaby that wasn't a lullaby anymore.

She turned it into a freaking weapon.

Another tunnel collapsed somewhere just beyond the room with the Isolation Vein, sending a puff of rock and dust spilling through the hole in the wall. "Not a lot of time." Nathan jumped to his feet.

"Go, go, go," Emily muttered, tugging furiously on the fragment of iron. "Don't stop, Nickie. I almost got it."

Nickie's mouth opened wide as her song reached a volume much louder than it should have been able to, even with the acoustics of a stone chamber. Emily's ears filled with a high, sharp ringing, her skull vibrating with a dull, heavy throb. She blinked thickly and tugged with everything she had on the iron shard, which slipped in her sweaty fingers.

Nathan clamped his hands over his ears as Nickie tipped her head back let out a long note that was more shriek than song. Stones fell from the ceiling, Emily was sure she was about to go deaf, and then the iron fragment popped loose with a brilliant purple flash.

The youngest Hadstrom sister toppled backward onto the floor and clutched the iron even tighter. "Let's go!"

She couldn't hear her own voice, but Nathan could. He lunged across the iron vein, snatched Nickie's hand, and yanked her to her feet. Emily scrambled after them and darted through the shattered doorway of Kashgar runes just before the room protecting the Isolation Vein crumbled behind her.

"Come on!" Nathan shouted, dragging Nickie back up the stairs. Emily booked it after them, slipping once on the slick surface before scrambling back to her feet and almost crawling the rest of the way on her hands and knees.

Nathan and Nickie both reached out and grabbed one of Emily's arms as the staircase gave way with an explosive boom. The ground shuddered again, and the trio stared up at the rock wall serving as the side of the creek bed keeping the waterfall on its current path. The wall split and started to buckle.

"Don't stop!" Nathan spun Nickie around and shoved her toward the thick woods away from the creek.

Emily hurried after, risking a glance over her shoulder to see Nathan close on her heels. And behind him, the side of the waterfall roared and crumbled, sending half of Barton Creek after them.

CHAPTER TWENTY-TWO

We can't outrun that.

Despite the thought flashing through her head, Emily's legs pumped faster than she would have thought they could. The only things she could hear were rumbling stone and crashing earth and water bursting through the trees. Wood splintered and cracked under the force of the unleashed water, and she waited for her racing feet to be swept out from under her any second now before the creek carried her away.

"Wha—"

At Nathan's shout behind her, Emily reacted and looked back. He was gone. She whirled back toward her sister and kept running, but Nickie had disappeared too.

"Nickie! Where—"

Emily's feet left the ground, but the force that had her didn't come from the water rushing below her. Strong hands gripped her under the arms and hoisted her into the air. Swaying branches thick with leaves whipped her face, and the next thing she knew, Emily was being pulled backward by her armpits along the thick, high branch of a live oak. When everything stopped moving, she turned back to see one of the Tree Folk holding her to his chest.

The being let out an apologetic chuckle and gently released her.

"Thanks." Her voice wobbled. "That was the last kind of rescue I was expecting. Not that I was expecting to be—"

A boulder crashed into the live oak's trunk, sending a shiver up the tree as the branches swayed. Emily threw herself at the branch she was straddling and wrapped her arms around it just to feel something relatively steady beneath her.

From somewhere on Emily's right, Nickie shouted, "We're safe up here, right?"

"Nickie?"

"Over here, Em!" Nickie clung to an overhanging branch in a huge tree a few yards away from Emily's. "You okay?"

"Yeah, just hangin' out!" Something else crashed into the live oak's trunk, and Emily gripped the branch tighter with her arms and her legs. A nervous laugh escaped her. "Not the time for bad tree puns, is it?"

A thin but much more lively female face belonging to one of the Tree Folk popped into Emily's line of vision. The being hung upside down by her long, thin tail and studied Emily, blinking large golden eyes. "You are quite safe up here," she said, her voice calm and soothing and surprisingly loud despite the rush of water passing beneath them. "As is your sister and the man with a Kashgars' eyes. When the flooding subsides, we will take you back to your box on wheels."

Emily snorted and forced herself not to look down at the muddy, churning flood beneath her. "We call it a car."

"Of course."

How did she manage to make that sound like I'm *the one who's lost touch with modern technology?* With a deep breath, Emily lifted her head and searched the treetops around her as well as she could for not being ready to let go of the branch beneath her. "Where *is* Nathan, by the way?"

Without taking her eyes from the youngest Hadstrom witch, the female creature pointed straight down the live oak's branch. In an adjacent tree, Nathan straddled a broad tree branch, but he sat upright against the trunk, his head tipped back against the rough bark and his eyes closed.

"So nobody got crushed underground or drowned by the flood. I guess it could be worse."

"Did you retrieve what you sought in that place?"

Emily had been clenching her fists so tightly, she couldn't feel the difference between the empty hand and the one wrapped around the shard of iron ore the size of a quarter. Carefully, she opened her right hand just enough to glance inside, then quickly tightened her grip again. The Tree Folk woman dangling beside her got enough of a glimpse to make her huge golden eyes grow even wider.

"Looks like it, yeah." Emily cleared her throat. "Sorry about the part where I detonated the creek with a dwarven hammer."

The monkey-like woman chuckled and shook her head. Thin tufts of golden-brown hair fluttered in the hot, humid air around her face. "You owe an apology to no one, Emily Hadstrom. A few holes beneath the earth are nothing compared to the devastation the gorafrex will leave on this ship and all its people should that being achieve what it desires."

"That's a relief, I guess." Finally, Emily let herself look down at the sloshing, flooded ground beneath her. The water level had already gone down quite a bit, and everything seemed to be floating back toward the creek bed. "Thanks for keeping an eye on us, by the way."

The female creature hanging beside Emily glanced at the male who'd pulled the young witch up into the tree. He spread his arms with shrug, then stood on the branch and leapt onto a bough overhead. "Not our eyes," the monkeylike woman muttered. "We heard your sister's magic. She is much stronger now than when the grackles led you to us for our first encounter."

"Can't argue with you on that one." With some hesitation, Emily let go of the branch she was hugging to push herself up. Her thighs ached with how hard she'd been squeezing the live oak's limb, but it was better than getting swept away by a flood. *Or losing this bit of iron that apparently takes way more than a little mining.*

She almost pressed herself back down against the branch when one of the Tree Folk swung through the air beside her. The furred woman landed squarely on the branch behind Emily with both feet, opposable thumbs and all. Then she let out another lighthearted chuckle and set a warm, gentle hand on the young witch's shoulder. "I can assure you that you were much more likely to be buried alive than you are to fall from this tree. Not while my people are here to see you safely on your way."

"Then the chances of being buried alive must've been pretty good." Steeling herself, Emily turned halfway around to look at the woman, then reached out with her empty hand to grasp her rescuer's hand. "You probably had no idea, but I'm not afraid of heights."

"That is fortunate." The woman helped Emily to her feet with a firm grip on the witch's hand, then led her charge back along the sprawling limb toward the live oak's trunk.

"Yeah." Emily's gaze dropped from the bough in front of her, and she jerked her head up to keep from seeing the gaping space of a dozen feet beneath her. "Only thing is, I think this is what being afraid of heights looks like. Or feels like."

They reached the center of the tree, and the woman guided Emily's hand to the rough bark covered in moss. A line of ants made their way down toward the forest floor. "You can let go of me now."

"Oh. Sorry." A wave of dizziness made Emily step as close as she possibly could to the trunk until she was once more hugging a pillar of wood. "This is super-weird."

"I imagine what you refer to as a fear of heights is, in reality, the energetic pull of that piece of iron in your hand."

"The iron's afraid of heights? Imagine that."

"The iron belongs to the earth and within it, Emily Hadstrom. That is where its purpose lies and to which it will always be called to return."

The young witch clenched her eyes shut, then opened them again, and saw Nickie already halfway down the live oak the Tree Folk had whisked her up into. "I guess that makes flying in planes a really bad idea."

"Beyond the fact that your family has vowed to remain

in this place you call Austin until the ship's voyage is complete? Yes. Planes are a bad idea."

"Where's Emily?" Nathan asked from somewhere on the ground.

"She was just— Okay, Em. Quit playing around in the tree. It's time to go."

"I'm not playing around in the—" Emily grunted and shook her head. "I just need a minute!"

"You okay?"

"I'm being energetically pulled to the earth. Or something."

"What?"

The monkey-like woman who'd led Emily this far gave the witch a sympathetic smile, then dropped from the adjacent branch and disappeared.

With her sister, Nathan, and most of the Tree Folk who'd come to their rescue standing on the sodden ground below her, Emily's urge to get her feet back on solid ground grew even stronger. "I'm coming."

CHAPTER TWENTY-THREE

Surrounded by almost a dozen of the Tree Folk on the ground, Nickie stepped toward her sister and wrapped her arm around Emily's shoulders with a grin. "That was insane. You okay?"

"Yep. Even with my shoes full of water." A wet squelch sounded at Emily's next step, and she let out a heavy sigh.

"You look a little pale."

"Just trying to brush off the vertigo." Emily opened her hand enough to show her sister the shard of iron nestled in her palm. "This thing doesn't like being off the ground."

"Huh. I hope it doesn't have an issue with being part of a potion."

"Well, it was forged into legacy rings and a massive underground prison. I'm pretty sure being dropped into a few other mixed ingredients won't be that big a deal." Emily nodded at Nathan. "You good?"

"I think so, yeah." He gestured toward the Tree Folk standing around them. "Thanks to all of you."

"We're lucky you followed us out here from the tree in the creek," Nickie added.

"They didn't," Emily whispered.

"What?"

The monkey-like woman who'd helped Emily down the live oak, dressed in a dark-green jumpsuit that looked like it was made of leaves, stepped toward them and gave a little bow. "We merely answered the call."

"The…" Nickie's lips twitched into a confused smile, and she turned toward her sister without looking away from the female creature in front of them. "What's she talking about?"

"Your song," another of the Tree Folk replied. This one's fur was as dark as the tree bark around them, his eyes glinting a deep brown flecked with gold. "The first was truly a boon for us, Nickie Hadstrom. A bit of kindness and healing. We are grateful."

"Of course. It was the least I could do."

"And it reconnected us to smaller pieces of magic still intact within the chaos." The creature grinned, and his female counterpart continued.

"The magic you worked below the earth is something else entirely," she said. "Not just a tool for undoing the grounding element of your ancestors' work, but for empowering the forces around you into something far beyond what they otherwise would have been."

Nickie licked her lips and stared at the Tree Folk like they were playing a joke on her instead of offering her strange, meaningful riddles. "So, my music. You're saying it healed you by the river. And then?"

The Tree Folk closed in around the Hadstrom sisters

and Nathan, and their female spokesperson dipped her eyes toward Nickie, her eyes wide and enlivened. "You healed us by the river. And then you readied us to fight." The woman snapped her fingers, and the entire party—Tree Folk and all—disappeared from the sodden ground on the other side of the creek.

When they reappeared miles downriver and just a few minutes' hike from the parking lot, Emily and Nickie both gasped in surprise. Emily gripped her sister's wrist and stared straight ahead at nothing, hoping the feeling would stay with her for longer than a few brief seconds. "Did you feel that?"

Nickie's nod was almost imperceptible. "Magic at full force, Em."

Though they'd whispered, the Tree Folk heard the short conversation. "Not at its fullest yet," their leader replied. "Not quite. But we have enough of it now to offer you whatever help you might need from us. Which, I imagine, will be quite soon."

Emily blinked. "Did she just fix magic?"

The male with the bright-green eyes shook his head. "No. She merely directed it into a channel that is much easier for us to access. The Tree Folk have long memories, yes. We remember the last time such a call was raised for our help. The Hadstrom magicals who created those rings offered very much the same songs when they prepared for battle with the gorafrex."

Nickie couldn't help but chuckle, even under the fierce pressure of her sister's fingers digging into her arms. "I inherited the same magic. Not just the legacy or the ring."

"And not just insane musical skills, apparently," Emily muttered. "We thought those came from Dad."

"And from whom do you suppose your father received his gift?" The Tree Folk chuckled, whispering to each other and taking to the trees again until the only two left standing in front of the Hadstrom sisters were those who'd been speaking. "Magic is tied to this ship and the mechanisms powering the organic life. The sentience. It would be foolish to think that a few broken pieces would strip the magic entirely from any people who have survived the journey so far."

"You mean the energy cores," Emily said. "That's why nothing's working the way it's supposed to. The gorafrex powered a few of them, and now…"

"The magic of our old homes, our true homes beyond the stars, still thrives," the male leader added. "The body might forget, but magic does not. Thank you both for reminding us all of that truth. Now we are hale enough to stand by your side. Do not forget as we did."

Emily stared with wide eyes at the glowing particles of the male creature's fur around his face. A breeze picked up, ruffling everyone's hair, and it looked like magic was up and running again. "I don't think that's possible to forget."

"Thank you," Nickie added. "Hopefully, we won't have to bring anyone else into this again when we find the gorafrex. Hopefully, we don't need your help. But if we do—"

"Then you know how to ask for it." The female leader of the Tree Folk grinned and bowed toward each of the magicals her people had saved from the flooding waterfall. The next second, both creatures disappeared into the thick canopy of the Greenbelt's trees. The only proof that they hadn't teleported again was the swing and sway of the branches before a handful of leaves fluttered to the forest floor.

"Wow." Nickie stared into the canopy. "Looks like we're repeating history, huh?"

Nathan turned in a slow circle and stared into the trees. "Well, that's what happens when it's been forgotten."

"You know what would be cool?" Emily muttered. "If the Hadstrom who made *my* ring was some kinda potions master."

"It seems a lot more likely now, Em."

"Yeah, it does. Hey, what about Laura, then? Did she get her archaeology skills from the Hadstrom who made *her* ring?"

Nickie snorted and nodded toward the footpath a few yards away through the trees. "Probably not what archaeology is right now, but there might've been something about artifacts."

"Or weapons."

Both Hadstrom sisters paused and turned to stare at Nathan.

"What? That's not obvious to you guys?"

"Oh, yeah. It's totally obvious." Emily squinted at him. "We just wanna hear why *you* came to that conclusion."

He shot them a half-smile and shrugged. "You guys have all those iron weapons, right? The lance. The daggers. Those little flying balls on a string."

Emily barked a laugh and trudged toward the footpath. "I only have one of those now, but yeah. I still need to settle on a good name for those. Flying balls on a string doesn't cut it."

"Well, whatever they are, Laura told me her ring made them, not her. Or I guess not intentionally."

Nickie stepped over a fallen log and ducked under the overhanging branches of a poplar sapling as Emily held them aside. "Right. That was before we officially connected with the rings, I guess."

"And that didn't last nearly long enough before magic broke and the rings stopped doing their thing." Emily waited for Nathan to step past her before letting the tree branches swing back into place.

"That's what I'm saying," Nathan added. "Maybe the Hadstrom who made Laura's ring was a weaponsmith of some kind."

"That feels kind of ironic, though. Laura the weapon-smith, whose secret alter ego collects every magical artifact she finds *and* can't stand the idea of magical creatures having to fend for themselves in the wild, so she takes them home."

"It's not impossible to be a warrior and compassionate at the same time, Em."

"Oh, yeah. I know. I just hope that when we finally find her and get her away from the gorafrex, Laura doesn't have a sudden change of heart and decide she feels sorry for the thing. I'm cool with all the other creatures stowed in her closet, but that would be crossing a line."

"That thing fought your dog and then kidnapped her," Nathan said. "I'm pretty sure your sister knows what you guys are up against."

"Yeah, but a gorlek and the gorafrex are two totally different things."

"And yet…" Emily laughed as the trio returned to the footpath and headed downriver toward the parking lot. "Nickie Hadstrom has the ability to sing them both into submission."

"Warrior musician." Nickie shook her head. "It's a little weird, but I guess I'm gonna have to accept it."

"Yep." The youngest Hadstrom sister opened her clenched fist enough to see the shard of iron they'd pulled from the Isolation Vein, then she carefully put their final ingredient in her front pocket and patted it. "And we're about to head into battle."

CHAPTER TWENTY-FOUR

"Chucky, we're home."

Nickie slid past her sister through the front door and shot Emily a squinting glance of disapproval. "Maybe you should quit while you're ahead."

"What? That's not how anyone improves, Nickie. You get better by pushing and pushing some more."

"Until your sense of humor breaks, right?" Nathan closed the front door behind him and laughed.

"Aw, come on. You too? I thought you liked my jokes." Emily slipped out of her wet, squelching sneakers and peeled off her soaked socks.

"Hey. How did it go?" Chuck rounded the corner out of the dining room, hands covered in Emily's matching oven mitts. Yellow-brown powder stained his t-shirt toward the bottom, and both his face and the roots of his blond hair were smudged with soot.

Emily grinned and looked him over. "About the same as it went for you, looks like."

Nickie slid her arms around her boyfriend's neck and kissed him. "Just glad to be home."

Chuck blinked at her, then removed his hands from her waist. "You're all wet."

"Yeah, Barton Creek underwent a little remodeling."

"What?"

Emily headed for her makeshift potions lab on the dining room table and tossed them a dismissive wave over her shoulder. "Technically, we *could* blame Carl's tiny hammer and not the witch who used it to crack through the wards on the Isolation Vein. But semantics, right?"

Chuck glanced at Nathan, who'd finally gotten his shoes off at the front door and shrugged. "Accidental demolition. Under a waterfall."

"But everything's fine," Nickie added, cupping Chuck's cheek. "We got what we needed."

"Thanks to the Tree Folk! Hey, Chuck. Would you believe Nickie's music magic splits pure iron *and* calls nearly immortal magicals to ready for battle? Oh, plus healing and then fighting off the gorafrex. Major Valkyrie material, if you ask me."

"I have no response for that."

Nickie grinned. "That's okay. So, how did it go with the potion?"

When she left him for the dining room table, Chuck turned toward her and opened his mouth but completely forgot what he'd wanted to say. "Fine. I think. I mean, nothing awful happened, so I'm pretty sure I did it right. Right?"

"Looks good to me." Emily studied the recipe on her

phone, glanced at the mixing bowl in front of her—now filled with a bright yellow liquid that looked like it needed to be flushed down the toilet—and nodded. "Before I make any judgment calls, wanna tell me why you're wearing oven mitts and have ash all over your face?"

Chuck cleared his throat. "The, uh, some of those things explode when you mix 'em."

"They do, huh?"

"I thought I'd burned my eyebrows off the first time, so I figured I'd go the safety route and…" He stopped and finally noticed both of the Hadstrom sisters staring at him with barely concealed smiles. "You knew I was going to almost blow myself up, didn't you?"

"No, Chuck. I knew you *wouldn't* blow yourself up."

Nickie cocked her head and squinted at her boyfriend. "I can honestly say I had no idea those ingredients would explode."

"And nobody would've let the guy try his hand at potions if I'd said anything." Emily tossed her hands up and let out an exaggerated sigh. "It's like nobody trusts me."

"I didn't have a problem with it." Chuck slipped his hands out of the oven mitts and rubbed a hand over his soot-dusted hair. "Just some sparks in a clear bowl, right? And a *tiny* bit of blue fire. But it went out, so…"

"That's the point I was trying to make." Emily clapped a hand on his shoulder and gave him a little shake. "You *got* this, Chuck. We do need you, and this is the best possible way you could've helped us. So well done."

"Yeah, okay." He tried not to look too proud of himself.

"She's right." Nickie slipped her hand into his and

patted his chest with the other hand. "You saw how many times Laura and I had issues with following the recipes."

"Yeah, Nathan and I ended up wearing most of those issues. Kinda hard to forget."

"Well, if Emily Hadstrom says you mastered a potion, it would be stupid not to believe her."

"Woah, woah, woah. Let's not get ahead of ourselves. I didn't say anything about *mastering* a potion." Emily winked at them, then pulled the shard of iron from her front pocket and held it up to the light. "So much craziness for a little hunk of rock."

"How did you find it, anyway?" Chuck asked.

Nickie gestured toward Nathan. "We had a part-Kashgar guide. And he did a great job."

Nathan folded his arms. "Guess the Hadstrom sisters graduated from needing guinea pigs to having sidekicks."

"Sidekicks." Chuck snorted and put his arm around Nickie's shoulders.

"Okay, everybody. Moment of truth right here."

Emily held the iron shard just over the bowl of her almost-finished potion, then plopped it in. Instantly, a thick foam boiled up toward the edge of the bowl, hissing and bubbling and flashing bright silver light like a growing lightning storm. Everybody stepped away from the table and waited.

"Is it supposed to do that?" Nathan asked.

Emily wrinkled her nose. "I have no clue. The recipe is for bringing parts of a whole back together, but I'm assuming it's different for every whole."

The mixing bowl lurched on the table, sending the thick foam sloshing over the sides. Instead of spilling out onto the table, though, the foam shot into the air, hovered a few feet above the bowl, and with a little pop, disappeared. The potion left behind was a thick, shimmering gray settling calmly back into place.

"Hey, look at that." Laughing, Emily grabbed the edge of the table and leaned forward until she was staring through the side of the bowl at eye level. "Magical quicksilver."

"That the final step, Em?"

"Yep."

"Okay. Time to gear up." Nickie slipped her hand out of Chuck's and turned toward the living room. Emily darted past the guys and stormed up the stairs toward her room.

"Gear." Chuck turned to Nathan raised his eyebrows. "They have gear we haven't seen yet?"

The physics professor shook his head. "I've given up trying to figure out what they're thinking. It's like they can read each other's minds."

"*Thank you.*" Chuck sighed and scratched the soot streaks on his jaw. "I've been thinking that for years."

Nathan stuck out his fist, and Chuck bumped it just before Nickie stepped back into the foyer with her dark-blue Strat strapped over her shoulder and the new portable amp in her other hand.

"Woah. You goin' on tour without me, babe?"

"Very funny." She stepped toward him and kissed him long enough to make Nathan turn back toward the dining room and stare at the ceiling. "You got me this brand-new amp, and I'm gonna break it in."

"Hopefully not the same way you broke the last one." He chuckled and glanced at the amp. "It was the only one I could get without waiting weeks for shipping, and I wasn't sure about it. When you're holding it like that, though, red might be your new color."

Nickie snorted.

"Oh, yeah." Emily skipped down the stairs two at a time. "Does it match her eyes, Chuck?"

"Man, I hope not."

"Uh, Em?"

"You don't have to comment." The youngest Hadstrom sister reached the bottom of the stairs and spread her arms to showcase her newest piece of battle gear. "It's perfect. I know."

"You're wearing a fly-fishing vest."

"Yep."

"From what? Seventh grade?" A laugh burst out of Nickie, then she squinted at the other vest dangling from Emily's outstretched hand. "And a backup, huh?"

"No, it's for you."

"I feel like I'm missing something." Chuck gestured from one vest to the other. "You guys put some kinda protection spell on those? Like armor or something?"

"No, but good idea for later." Emily pointed at him, then held the second vest out toward her sister. "Put it on, Nickie, and I'll show you how it works."

"Where did you even find these?" Nickie set down the amp, lifted her guitar strap over her head, and handed the instrument to Chuck without looking away from her new battle-witch getup.

"In my closet. Last night was a lesson in how *not* to run around Austin with a bunch of potions. Namely, rolled into an apron where they get all confused."

"And you just happened to have two fishing vests in your closet." Nickie grabbed the vest and slipped it on.

"Tada! Makes me wonder how close Dad took me to the prison whenever we went to the Greenbelt to catch a few."

"Feels more ironic than it probably should."

"I know, right?" Emily adjusted the sides of her sister's vest and spread her fingers wide to showcase her excitement. "Check this out. Left top pocket is for getting back home. Right top pocket for getting right into the Clubhouse without our keyrings. Bottom left, you got what I like to call erasers—"

"Sounds like a euphemism."

Emily peered over her sister's shoulder to shake her head at Nathan as he joined them in the foyer. "If I was gonna pick a euphemism for something, it would be a heck of a lot cooler than a school supply. There are three in that pocket, Nickie. They'll get through simple wards and maybe alarm charms, and they *should* do something to help with any magical damage to…well, to us. Not that you need healing potions, right? Just sing the wound closed."

Chuck exhaled. "See, I was totally on board with Operation Save Laura until you brought up wounds."

"Don't worry about it. Nickie healed the magic right back into the Tree Folk. Trust me, they did not look good when we saw them today."

Chuck shot Nathan a curious glance, and the professor muttered, "People who look like monkeys and live in the trees."

"Right."

"Besides, we've been out plenty of times before *and*

since you found out what we are, Chuck. And I don't remember any of us getting seriously hurt."

Nickie nodded absently, patting the pockets of Emily's vest. "Just the human hosts. But I healed them too, so… Hey, what's in this pocket?"

"Don't!" Emily lurched forward and caught Nickie's hand in both of hers. The sisters shared a wide-eyed glance as Emily slowly pulled Nickie's hand out to the side and shook her head. "That's one of the bombs."

"Bombs."

"Seriously?" Chuck clutched the Strat tighter to his chest until he realized what he was doing and forced himself to loosen up.

"Why did you give me an explosive potion you're afraid of?"

"Because…" Emily smoothed the other pockets of Nickie's vest and felt way too much like their mom getting them ready for elementary school. So she folded her arms and stepped back. "Because I don't have enough pockets to carry everything I made, and I don't wanna leave anything behind."

"Fair enough. How 'bout we trade, though? You take the bomb in a vial, and I'll take whatever you've got that doesn't have 'Emily likes to blow things up' written all over it."

The youngest Hadstrom sister threw her head back and laughed. "I gave you the least dangerous one, Nickie. Just don't touch it, and we'll live to rescue Laura." She cleared her throat and double-checked all the other pockets of her vest. The vials clinked against each other under her hands, and she grinned. "So, we're set."

"You need to take that last one with you?" Chuck asked as Nickie took her guitar from him again and ducked through the strap.

"Nope." Emily rubbed her hands together and went back to the dining room table. "We get to use this one before we take off. Thanks to you, Chuck. You saved us at least an hour. You rock."

"You were gone for almost two hours."

Nickie glanced at him. "Did it take you two hours to put everything together?"

"Babe, I wasn't gonna rush through my first real potion in your house, by myself, when magic doesn't work even though I don't know how to use it." For the first time since the witches and the professor had returned from the Greenbelt, Chuck looked more than a little proud of himself. "So, yeah. I took my time. That's how you make sure things get done right."

Emily laughed. "Totally. I'm glad you found your groove. Okay." She rifled through the red bucket on the table with all the supplies she'd collected and pulled out a glass dropper. "Get over here, Nickie. I don't wanna drop this stuff anywhere."

"And that's because…"

"I have no idea what it would do. To the table, the floors, a hand…"

Nathan shoved his hands into his pockets and chewed the inside of his bottom lip, keeping a sharp gaze on the dropper Emily lowered into the bowl of iron-grounded potion. "And that is why it makes perfect sense that potions fell off the list of things to learn as a magical. A simple spell is a simple spell. Even when it goes wrong, the worst that can happen is you can't stop conjuring flowers, or you end up turning a mouse into a dog instead of trapping it."

Emily shot him a confused look. "That happen to you?"

"No. Just random examples."

"I'll take the unknown risk of potions right now over not having any kind of reliable magic." Nickie stopped beside her sister and glanced at the black legacy ring on her thumb. "Gives us an advantage over pretty much everyone."

"Except for the witch-killer we're trying to take down and lock up." Emily paused at the reminder of the gorafrex using potions too, then shook her head. "That doesn't matter. My potions are better anyway."

"You're sure of that?" Chuck asked.

"Of course, I'm sure. It's in my blood." Emily dipped the dropper into the viscous silver potion, squeezed the rubber tip, and made a face when an air bubble moved through the liquid with a thick, burbling slowness. Then she lifted the dropper back out and nodded at Nickie. "This goes on our rings, so get your hand as close to the bowl as you can. Safety first and all that."

Nickie snorted. "You are *really* drawing out the suspense."

"Why not?" With her tongue poking out between her lips in concentration, Emily slowly moved the dropper toward her sister's hand. "Just a few—"

Nickie jerked her hand away, and the huge silver drop fell onto the polished wood of the dining room table with a tiny pop. It left a dent in the soft wood, rippled in the resulting hole for a second, then evaporated.

"*Nickie.* Now's not the time to test how steady my

hands are." Emily looked at her sister and froze. "No. Really? Right now?"

Gritting her teeth, Nickie rubbed her forehead just above her eye, then lurched back and doubled over. The gorafrex's ancient, primal drumbeat flared in her head and blocked out every other sound, including her voice when she whispered, "We're running out of time, Em."

CHAPTER TWENTY-FIVE

"The drums are back." Emily emptied the dropper back into the bowl of grounding potion and tossed the glass tube onto the baking tray. "Okay. On a scale of one to ten, Nickie, how bad is it?"

"Really?"

"How bad?"

"Like a seven. Eight." Nickie groaned and managed to swing her Strat into her arms before she leaned against the wall beside the kitchen. "So, either the gorafrex has to find a new host right now, or it's already got Laura where it wants her. And it's gonna—"

"Nope. That's not an option. Got it?" Emily went to her sister and grabbed Nickie's shoulders to get her attention. Nickie's eyes were clenched shut, though, and she didn't open them. "Can somebody get her some water, please?"

"Yeah." Chuck all but ran past them into the kitchen, throwing open cabinet doors and slamming them shut again because he couldn't remember where the Hadstrom sisters kept their glasses.

"We can still go right now," Emily said, squeezing Nickie's shoulders. "If you say you can handle it and you think you can shred the hell out of that guitar the minute we get there, we can do this."

"No, we can't, Em." Nickie let out a long, heavy breath through her nose. "We can't fight that thing without Laura. And she doesn't have what *she* needs."

"That stupid lance. It's in the Clubhouse, isn't it?"

Neither of them needed an answer to that question.

Emily hissed and spun away from her sister, giving Chuck the perfect opportunity to hand Nickie the glass of water and smooth the hair away from her forehead. "Okay. We need to get all the weapons from the Clubhouse too. I never thought I'd say I hate magic. Right now, I do."

"What about jumper cables?" Nathan offered.

Chuck looked up and glared at him. "Are you crazy?"

"Right." Emily slapped Chuck's arm with the back of her hand. "He's talking about a power boost. We used it to get to the Isolation Vein, and it helped fight off the greenhouse. Nickie, you have your keys?"

"Yeah." Clearing her throat and fighting off the pain bursting through her skull along with the gorafrex's urgent, rapid drumbeat, Nickie reached for her back pocket. Chuck helped her when she fumbled with the keys, and she gripped the silver Clubhouse coin in both hands to steady herself. "Ready."

"Awesome. This better work." Emily took out her keys, found the silver charm with her thumbprint etched into it, and reached for Nickie's hand.

A second before their fingers touched, Nickie disappeared.

Chuck stumbled forward, caught himself against the wall, and blinked. "I don't think I'm gonna get used to that."

"Seriously?" Emily thumbed her Clubhouse coin, but nothing happened. "She just—" Pressing her thumb over and over onto her thumbprint with no effect. The youngest Hadstrom sister spiked her keys onto the dining room floor and folded her arms. "Must've just missed the window."

"The Tree Folk did say magic was still floating around in small pockets," Nathan offered.

"Yeah, but it's not supposed to separate us." Emily gestured to the empty space where her sister had just been. "Now Nickie's in the Clubhouse with no guarantee that she'll be able to get back out when she's ready. It took her half an hour last time, and I'm here by myself. No jumper cables, no Hadstrom sisters, just Emily. Awesome."

With a grunt, the youngest Hadstrom sister stormed across the foyer and into the living room, muttering to herself. Nathan and Chuck exchanged glances, and Chuck bent to pick the keyring up off the floor. Nails clicked across the hardwood floor upstairs, heralding Speed's arrival. The immortal bulldog took his own sweet time coming down the steps, but when he reached the bottom, he stopped in the foyer to eye the Peabrain and the professor in the dining room.

"You know this dog pretty well, right?" Nathan muttered.

"Yeah. At least, I thought I did. Had no clue he turned into a snarling, six-foot fighting machine until this morning."

Nathan didn't take his eyes off the chubby bulldog

standing perfectly still beside the stairs. "Yeah, knowing that, I can't help but think it looks like he's blaming us for something."

Chuck cocked his head. "I can't help but agree with you."

Speed licked his jowls, let out a belch, and turned away from them to trot into the living room after Emily. He didn't roll over and beg for a belly rub as usual, but instead crawled into his charge's lap. Emily sat on the floor with her back against the overturned couch and didn't move when the added weight settled on her legs.

Clutching the keys tighter, Chuck stepped across the foyer and tried to gauge the level of Emily's reaction.

"If you wanna leave right now, I'm not gonna stop you," Emily muttered. "Who knows what I'm gonna ruin next if I get too upset? And I don't... I don't even know what I'm feeling right now."

Chuck took a deep breath and gazed around the mess Speed's fight with the gorafrex the night before had made of their living room. Nothing rattled on shelves or flew across the room. Nothing made a sound beyond Speed's contented panting in Emily's lap. "I'm gonna go ahead and take my chances, Em. The thing that took Laura scares me. Magic and potions and you guys disappearing and reappearing without warning. Yeah, that kind of scares me too. You don't."

"Great. Thanks. I'm a force to be reckoned with, huh?" She closed her eyes and sighed, but she finally lifted her hand to scratch behind Speed's ears. The dog settled his chin on her thigh and echoed her sigh.

"I know you don't like being wrong, but I have to call

you out on it." Chuck paused a few feet from the youngest Hadstrom witch, waiting for her to shoot him that look that meant she knew he was full of it. Emily didn't move, so he sat down in front of her and eyed Speed. The dog didn't move either. "It's not just you, Em."

She scoffed and dropped her hand from Speed's head. "Unless you can summon my sisters into this room from the Clubhouse and wherever Laura is, nice try."

"We're here." Nathan stopped inside the entryway to the living room and leaned against the wall. "And neither of us is going anywhere."

"That's a sweet thing to say, I guess." Emily opened her eyes and looked at Chuck sitting in front of her, then glanced at Nathan. "But despite what my sisters might think sometimes, I don't need a babysitter, let alone two."

"Nope." Chuck lifted Emily's keyring and gave it a shake. "Just friends. A part-Kashgar who knows how to find a bunch of steel underground—"

"Iron," Nathan corrected.

"*Iron*. And if it makes you feel better, there's a human right here who's useless with magic but might make a pretty decent apprentice."

"A potions apprentice." Emily blinked slowly and stared at him. "Seriously?"

"I mean, I guess I just assumed that apprentices are a thing. Is that not…"

"I mean, they're old-school." She shrugged and took the keys from him. "So are potions, so maybe it's a good fit."

"Just puttin' it out there." He grinned at her and nodded. "But the point is, even without your sisters, you're not useless, Em. And you're not alone."

"We have no idea how to help unless somebody tells us what needs to happen." Nathan stood from against the wall and took a few steps toward them. "I can't speak for Nickie's manager, but even if I wasn't on board with helping you get Laura back, I don't have anywhere else to be."

With a halting laugh of surprise, Chuck turned and frowned up at the tall professor. "Let's see. My best friend who owns a record label was possessed by the thing that took Laura and has his magic to deal with. No gigs for Nickie because we were supposed to be recording right now after signing a deal, and she's not here." He looked at Emily again with a crooked smile. "I'll have to check my schedule, Em, but I'm pretty sure I can squeeze in some time to help you. Somewhere."

Emily pressed her lips together and gazed at her sisters' boyfriends. "Okay. I can't say either one of you made especially convincing arguments, but I wanna stop this before it gets any mushier."

"Hey, I can go mushier if I have to."

"No, thanks." Emily gently nudged Speed off her lap. The dog didn't get up so much as he oozed off her legs onto the floor, but she patted his head anyway and stood. Chuck got to his feet, and the living room fell silent. Emily rubbed her hands together, looked around the room, and nodded. "Okay. Until I can screw my head back on straight, I'm gonna take you guys up on that offer and put you to work."

"Hey, if you need more potions, I'm your guy." Chuck stuck his thumb toward his chest and cocked his head. "Outsourcing, right?"

"When I have more potions to make, you're the first

person on my list of one, buddy." Emily nodded curtly and glanced at Nathan. "For now, while I wait for Nickie to pop out of the Clubhouse again or for a good idea to pop into my head, whichever comes first, I have a job for you guys."

"Great." Nathan nodded.

Chuck spread his arms. "At your service, Hadstrom."

"Awesome. Can you guys put the living room back together? I'm gonna go sauté something and hope it calms me down." Emily shoved her keyring into her back pocket and disappeared into the mudroom that led to the kitchen.

Chuck let out a disbelieving laugh and called after her, "You're just using us for our brute strength, huh?"

"That's it." Emily's voice floated through the mudroom, accompanied by banging cabinet doors. "You nailed it. Thanks!"

He scratched his head and gazed around the living room. "Definitely not what I had in mind."

"We gave her a wide-open shot on that one." Nathan bent beside the one armchair that hadn't been busted apart by a flying weredog in hot pursuit of a gorafrex and pulled it upright. "I'm taking a guess. She's the one who bottles everything up, huh?"

"Yep." With another wry chuckle, Chuck stepped toward the overturned coffee table on the rug scrunched against the wall and started to pull it all back into place. "Maybe blowing stuff up with potions will be a good outlet."

"Yeah, maybe."

CHAPTER TWENTY-SIX

Nickie took a deep breath and placed her hands on the rug beneath her. "Right idea. Bad timing." Now that she'd been whisked into the Clubhouse—once magic had decided to work for the half-second she had her thumb on her silver coin—the gorafrex's drumbeats were gone. A little bit of the headache remained, but it was nothing in comparison.

Picking up the glass of water, she drained the rest of it in one breath and didn't care that it fell over when she set it down again. "Okay. I'm here. With my guitar. Probably stuck in the Clubhouse until magic wants to let me out again. Sorry, Em. I honestly didn't think that would—"

The flutter of crinkling paper drew closer, and Nickie turned to see one of their origami animals before it smacked her in the face. Flinching away, she blinked and reached for the magically animated bit of paper in her lap. "You know, when we made you guys, there was nothing in the spell that said you had to throw yourselves at us every chance you..."

The paper jellyfish twitched in her hand, its stringy tentacles waving. The thing's body was crunched, like someone had crumpled it up to throw it away, but what made Nickie pause was the handwriting scrolling across the jellyfish in bright red Sharpie. "We definitely didn't draw on these."

She shifted onto her knees and spread the jellyfish flat on the rug. "What? She was here?" A sharp laugh escaped her, and she scanned the note one more time, still in too much disbelief to read any of the words or make them make sense in her head. But it was Laura's handwriting. "How did she pull *that* off?"

Her lingering headache was ignored as Nickie pushed herself to her feet and took the jellyfish note with her. Then she forced herself to focus on what it said.

At BWEmp now. Leo's here. G knows potions. Tenebantur! Two cores left, Oak Hill and Emma Long. Leave the lance. Bring____

The rest of the last word slipped away in a streak of red ink. Nickie stepped around the cherry-red futon, searching the Clubhouse for anything else Laura might have left them. The only thing that looked remotely different was the red Sharpie on the floor, its lid still lying on the kid-sized desk against the wall.

"Okay. She was here, and she left us a note." Once she remembered to start breathing again, Nickie let herself laugh one more time before stuffing the origami jellyfish note into her back pocket, followed quickly by her keys. Then she picked her Strat up off the rug and strapped it on again. "We need to be ready."

She went quickly to the tall bookshelf on the adjacent

wall and nodded at the iron weapons Laura's ring had made for them. That felt like two years ago instead of two weeks. The daggers, Laura's lance with the rune at the tip, and Emily's last remaining iron orb that tied its targets up in a web of iron string sat on the shelves. Nickie grabbed everything but the lance. "Yeah, she knows what she's doing, even though we have zero guarantee that she'll be able to get back here to— Nope. Gotta trust a note left on a jellyfish."

With her arms full, Nickie decided it was best to sit on the floor and pile everything into her lap, just to be sure she didn't leave anything behind the next time magic burst back on for however long. Then she pulled her keys from her pocket again and pressed her thumb firmly into its imprint on her Clubhouse coin. "It would *really* be great if we could hurry this up. I don't know if talking to magic is a thing, but if I had to talk to anything I can't see, you're the best choice right now. My sisters need me, and everyone else on this entire ship needs us. So, anytime. No pressure or anything, but we need to—"

The magical lights strung through the Clubhouse flared to a blinding brilliance, and Nickie closed her eyes. Something tugged on her like a hook caught in the center of her chest, and then she was gone.

When she popped back into the dining room, the iron orb toppled out of her lap and hit the floor with a thud before rolling toward the wall.

"What the—" Emily jumped and whirled away from the stove, raising her spatula in attack mode. "Nickie!"

"Em, she was there!" Nickie whipped the guitar strap over her head again, dropped everything else onto the floor, and leapt to her feet. "I mean, I didn't see her, but—"

The lit burner on the stove burst with flames two feet high, and the sauté pan full of Emily's attempt at lunch went flying. The pan clanged into the cabinets, and vegetables splattered everywhere. Emily chucked her spatula into the sink and jerked the burner's knob to off, then had to turn on the sink and use the adjustable spray hose to beat the flames down. The kitchen filled with a startling hiss, and Emily didn't even bother to put the hose back or turn off the faucet before she launched herself at her sister and wrapped Nickie in a crushing embrace.

"I thought I was gonna have to sit here for days without being able to see or talk to either of you."

"We got lucky." Nickie squeezed her back, then pried herself out of her little sister's arms and reached into her back pocket. "And so was Laura."

"Yeah, you said— Wait. She was in the Clubhouse?"

"*Yeah*. Sometime between last night and ten minutes ago, obviously. But she left us a note."

"She…*ha*! She left us a note. She's okay!"

"Yeah, yeah. Em, just look at this. I already know what—"

"Hey, what's going on?" Nathan poked his head through the mudroom into the kitchen, then took a sharp breath. "Look who's back? That didn't take long."

"That's what *I* said." Emily nodded at the paper. "Keep going."

"Here." Nickie shoved the jellyfish note into Emily's hand when she saw Chuck stepping into the kitchen with wide eyes. "Miss me?"

"It was only like ten minutes." He crossed the kitchen and didn't let her say anything before grabbing her face and kissing her. "And yeah. I totally missed you. Mostly because we had no idea when you'd be able to get back."

"I almost lost it. Now I don't have to." Emily chuckled and uncrumpled the paper jellyfish. "Holy crap! She *did* get in there."

"Yeah, Em. And she told us exactly what we need to do."

"Okay. *Brightwing Emporium with Leonidas.* Yeah, we figured that out after the singing bowl's fireworks display. *Gorafrex using potions.* Yep. *Tenebantur?*"

"That's the part I didn't get." Nickie pulled Chuck's hands from her cheeks and returned to her sister. "As far as I know, it doesn't have anything to do with the other two energy cores."

"And we already knew there were still two left."

"Right. So maybe the Tenebantur has to do with the potions? I don't know. But the rest of this about leaving the lance, which I did, by the way."

"Good."

"I think the gorafrex is taking her to one of the last energy cores. Right now, probably. And she knew that would happen soon."

Emily froze and looked up from the note to grin at her sister. "She wants us to bring all the gear and get ready to fight the gorafrex and save her at the same time."

"Yeah. Then we can get rid of the other two energy cores and start working on building magic back up again."

"Yes! *Yes!*" Emily roared and pumped her fist in the air. "Who knew I'd be this happy that you got sucked into the Clubhouse without me?"

"Em, I didn't know it would—"

"I didn't know it would do that, either. Totally okay. It's not your fault, so let's just forget it happened. Except for the part where Laura left us a note on an origami jellyfish, and you just happened to find it. We get to finish this!"

"As soon as we figure out what Tenebantur is." Nickie ran a hand through her hair and took a step back to help herself settle down. "I don't wanna get that one wrong."

"Right. And she wrote '*Bring_____*' Bring what?"

With a shrug, Nickie shook her head. "I'm guessing that if it was super-important, she wouldn't have written it at the end, right?"

"True. Okay. I'm gonna check everything I have. All the pictures from the books at the library."

"Sure."

Emily stormed into the dining room to grab her phone off the table. "It's probably not a good idea to try our luck getting into the restricted section again, but Isabelle knows her stuff. Wanna call and see if they have anything on Tenebantur?"

"Yep."

"And Nathan?"

"Yeah?"

Emily pointed at him without looking away from her phone as she scrolled through her photos. "I forgot to turn off the water."

"Sure, Em." He met Chuck's gaze and widened his eyes, then only had to take one step on his long legs toward the sink before the running water stopped with a squeak of the faucet.

Chuck glanced at the stove and turned in a slow circle

around the kitchen. "Hey, weren't you cooking something? Oh. Never mind."

"Yeah, I'm not hungry." Emily stared at her phone, her eyes darting back and forth before she flipped to the next picture.

Nickie hurried into the living room with her phone pressed to one ear and her finger jammed into the other. "Yeah, hi. I know the restricted section isn't up and running right now, so I was hoping you might be able to help me track down some information. Yep. I want to know if you guys have any books about Tenebantur. Or if anyone there can tell me what it means. Yeah, no problem. I can wait."

Nodding, Chuck crossed the kitchen and picked up the still-hot sauté pan that might have left a charred ring on the cabinet where it had landed. He tossed it quickly into the sink, then grabbed a rag and got to work cleaning the onions, garlic, zucchini, and mushrooms off the floor, counters, and cabinets. Nathan grabbed the trashcan in the mudroom and brought it to the center of the kitchen.

"Whatever we can do to help, right?" Chuck dumped the first rag full of veggies into the trashcan and snorted.

"Something tells me those witches aren't bothered by food on the…everywhere."

"Not right now. You haven't heard Emily talk about her kitchen, have you?"

Nathan pulled another rag from the open drawer beside the sink and offered it to Chuck. "Can't wait."

CHAPTER TWENTY-SEVEN

"Every time." Emily glared at her phone, then set it on the table again despite wanting to chuck it across the house. "I get way too excited, and then I don't find what I'm looking for."

"Nothing at the library, either." Nickie crossed the foyer into the dining room again and shrugged. "Isabelle sounded upset that she hadn't heard of Tenebantur and couldn't find anything about it in their catalog."

"What about a Google search?"

Nickie clicked her tongue. "Yeah, she tried that too."

Gripping the edge of the table and hanging her head between her arms, Emily clenched her eyes shut and scrunched up her face. "Tenebantur. What's that *mean?*"

"She wouldn't have written it down if she didn't think we could figure it out."

"I *know.* So we're missing something. The gorafrex is using potions. Tenebantur, then two energy cores left. Maybe I should've eaten something. I can't think!"

"Wait. We should call Mom."

Emily groaned and rolled her head from side to side where it hung. "I'm not interested in trying to explain to her that we know what that note means—mostly. If we bring Mom into this, she's gonna start talking about all the different potions she thinks we need to— Oh."

"There it is." Nickie grinned and patted her sister's back. "Want me to call her?"

Laughing, Emily straightened and grabbed her phone. "I'll do it. Save you headache of being the messenger. Mom and I can talk in potions code directly." She pulled up her mom's number, pressed her phone to her ear, and nodded at Nickie. "Good idea."

"That's why we're doing this together, right? Someone's gotta remind you that you and Mom are more alike than you think."

Emily sighed and leaned against the edge of the table.

"This is Nancy."

"Hey, Mom. It's me."

"Did you find her?"

"No, not yet." Emily frowned at Nickie's confusing pantomime until she realized the one-sidedness of the conversation and put her phone on speaker.

"But she left us a note, Mom," Nickie added, bending toward the phone in Emily's open palm.

"A *note*? From before that thing took her?"

"Nope. After."

"How is that possible? Where is she?"

"Mom, hold on a sec." Nickie took a deep breath. "We don't have a lot of time, and we called you 'cause we need your help."

"Anything. What is it?"

Emily cocked her head. "Do you know what a Tenebantur is?"

There was a long silence on the other end of the line.

"Mom?"

"Where did you hear about that?"

The Hadstrom sisters exchanged a startled glance. "Laura wrote it down for us. But she didn't say what it is."

"I don't think she had time," Nickie added.

"Okay, we—" Nancy sighed and cleared her throat. "We shouldn't talk about this over the phone. Are you home?"

"Yeah."

"Emily, I'm gonna text you an address. Meet me there in twenty minutes, and I will show you what your sister was talking about."

"Sure."

"Twenty minutes, girls." Nancy paused again. "And be ready to get your sister out of there after we meet up. You won't have a lot of time after that."

"Sounds good. Thanks, Mom. Love you." Emily ended the call and nodded. Then her determined smile faded into a frown, and she blinked at the black screen in her hand. "She just said we wouldn't have a lot of time after we meet with her, didn't she?"

"Yep." Nickie stretched her fingers, which kept moving on their own in the chord progression she didn't want to think about playing until they stood in front of the gorafrex inside its human host. With Laura. "That sounded like she's trying to hide something."

"Well." Emily stuffed her phone into her back pocket and turned to scoop up the iron orb Laura's ring had made her. "We told her our secret. Seems fair that she's got one to share with us, huh?"

"Em, Mom knew about the gorafrex before we thought about telling her."

"Same difference. Here." Emily lifted her sister's Strat in one hand and the portable amp in the other. "We're suiting up and getting ready to rock. In your case, literally."

"Yeah, okay." Nickie accepted her musical-equipment-turned-magical-weapon before grabbing one of the iron daggers and handing it to her sister. "Not like we have a lot of extra hands after potions and guitars, but why not?"

"Always the best way to go about things." Emily stuck the iron orb under her arm, then bent to pick up the glove Laura had made to keep the youngest Hadstrom witch from shredding her hands with thin iron wires and pulled it on. She held the dagger toward Nickie, who tapped the tip of her iron blade against it. They turned to see Chuck and Nathan staring at them from the kitchen.

Chuck's mouth popped open as he tried to find the right words. "You guys look…"

"Ridiculous. We know. But the gorafrex doesn't give a crap about how we look. Which actually doesn't matter in any context." Emily stopped to grab an empty vial from the red bucket, which she filled with enough of their newest tracking potion to burn holes in the entire table. Then she pocketed the potion, snatched her phone up off the table, and headed for the door. "Thanks for everything, guys. This is on us now, so we'll call you when we're done. Whenever that is." The front door opened and shut again behind her.

Pursing her lips, Nickie stepped toward Chuck and nodded. "You were gonna say sexy, weren't you?

"What?" He laughed. "Not in front of your sister."

"Good call." She gave him a quick kiss, then adjusted her guitar strap. "We're gonna get her back."

"I know."

"We'll be here when you get back," Nathan said. "If that's cool."

"Absolutely. If you're staying, would you mind feeding Speed? Cup and a half out of the bag in the mudroom."

"No problem."

"Thanks." Nickie took off toward the foyer. "Maybe give him some extra snuggles too. He deserves it after last night. Oh, and it probably wouldn't hurt to set something out for the grackles. They're still in the side yard."

"Feed them what?" Nathan called behind her.

"I have no idea. Look it up. Thanks!" Nickie fumbled to keep a grip on everything and open the door at the same time, but she finally managed it and hurried out after Emily toward her car. "Can you—"

"I'll get the door." Chuck stepped into the foyer and looked outside as Nickie disappeared down the cement stairs down to the street. Then he closed the door, paused, and walked back into his girlfriend's kitchen.

Nathan stood beside the fridge with a beer bottle in each hand and offered one to Chuck. "We can feed animals and wait for the heroes to return. But with beer."

"That's the best thing I've heard all day."

CHAPTER TWENTY-EIGHT

Nickie parked on Bowman Avenue at the address their mom had texted Emily. "She wants us to meet her at someone's house?"

"Yeah, I thought that was weird too." Emily stuck her dagger in the glovebox and shut it again after Nickie did the same. "We know anyone who lives out here?"

"Not off the top of my head. But we *are* close to both of the last energy cores, so it's not a detour."

"Convenient." Emily unbuckled her seatbelt and got out of the car.

Before Nickie had shut the driver's door behind her, Nancy Milton pulled up behind them in her new Camry. It took their mom two seconds to jump out of her car, look her daughters up and down, and gesture toward the row of houses. "You two look like you're ready for…something."

"Right now, that's figuring out what the Teneba—"

"Not here, Em. Not yet." Nancy put an arm around her youngest's shoulders and led them up the cement pathway toward the designated house.

"Good to see you too."

"Mom." Nickie readjusted the strap of her guitar, feeling a little weird for having it over her head. *There's no such thing as being too careful right now.* "What are we doing here?"

"Visiting a friend."

"Is this friend dangerous?"

Emily nodded and studied their mom's profile. "Yeah, you're acting like this friend is dangerous."

"No. Just the information he has. Especially now, with everything being off."

"You mean magic." Nickie gazed at the beams over the front porch that looked like they would crash down under a strong wind.

"Magic, the gorafrex, and Austin being upside-down magically speaking, while only a handful of people know what's going on." Nancy removed her arm from Emily's shoulders and reached out to ring the doorbell. A loud, repetitive honk from a flock of geese sounded in response.

"What about this friend?" Emily ask. "Does he know about all that?"

"No, and none of us are going to tell him, okay?" Nancy took a deep breath, straightening her t-shirt.

"You look nervous," Nickie said.

"I do not."

Emily frowned at their mom and took a step away from her when Nancy reached out for the doorbell again. "Why won't you just tell us who we're meeting? We're not gonna judge."

"It's an old boyfriend, isn't it?"

"Nickie, I'm not gonna answer that question."

"A *new* boyfriend," Emily guessed, wiggling her eyebrows.

"Stop it."

"Only if you tell us what's going on."

Nancy sighed and closed her eyes. "I'm sure you'll hear all about it when we step inside."

"Not a boyfriend, but not somebody we know." Emily rubbed at her chin. "And you want to keep it a secret because…"

"Because he's my—"

The doorknob let out a grating squeal when it turned from the inside, and the first thing to greet them on the other side of the door was a terrifying round of hacking coughs and smoke that billowed out onto the porch.

Trying not to start coughing, Nancy waved a hand in front of her face and put on the fakest smile her daughters hadn't known she could master. "Astro."

"Heh? Huh? What?" Something moved behind the smoke, and the head that finally poked through into fresh air was a foot shorter than either of the Hadstrom sisters had expected. Huge silver eyes blinked quickly from behind ridiculously thick lenses, and a wrinkled hand grabbed the thick frames to readjust them. "I'm not interested."

The man retreated into the smoke and started to close the door, but Nancy grabbed it and held it open. "It's Nancy Milton. I know you remember me. These are my daughters, and we all need your help."

Nothing moved but the smoke was still spilling through the open door.

"Yeah, get in line." Then the crotchety old man disappeared into his house again.

Emily waved the smoke away from her face. "Um…"

"If you keep standing there like a bunch of solicitors, that's how I am to treat ya. Get inside and close the damn door."

"Huh." Nickie cocked her head. "Not a very nice friend, Mom."

"Come on." Nancy ignored her daughter's comment and stepped through Astro's front door before disappearing in the smoke.

Emily just shrugged and stepped inside. "You got the door?"

"Yeah. I got the door." Pulling a face at the smoke, which was acrid and sour and didn't smell like anything she could name, Nickie stepped inside and had to turn the doorknob extra hard to get it to unstick and latch behind her.

Then she couldn't see a thing. "Mom?"

"Nancy, you have three full-grown daughters, and you didn't teach them how to look without seeing. Hm. I'm surprised they can take care of themselves."

"Room on the left, Nickie," Nancy called.

Nickie followed her mom's voice, cradling her Strat to keep it from knocking into anything while reaching out through the smoke with her other hand. When she stepped through the doorway into said room, a strong breeze buffeted her hair, sending it fluttering into her eyes. She ducked, pulled hair out of her mouth and eyes, and looked around.

"And suddenly, she can see again." The old man sitting in an armchair across from Nancy thumped his cane on the floor with both hands and snorted. "Can't teach anyone anything."

Emily stood behind the armchair where their mom sat, and she nodded for Nickie to come stand on the other side of it. Nancy waited until both her daughters stood behind her, in full view of the man, who obviously didn't want visitors but couldn't say no. Then she spread her arms and gestured to her girls. "Astro, these are my daughters, Nickie and Emily Hads—"

"Where's the other one, eh?" Astro's magnified eyes twitched as he leaned forward and peered at Nancy. He didn't even try to meet the sisters' gazes. "What happened to her?"

"That's why we're here." Nancy took a deep breath. "Laura was taken last night. We have an idea of where she is, and we—"

"Oh, you have an *idea*, do ya?" Astro cocked his head until his huge, protruding ear almost touched his shoulder. "*You* have an idea, Milton? Or *they* do?"

"Fine." Nancy leaned back in the armchair, crossed one ankle over the opposite knee, and spread her arms. "They're all yours."

"What?" Nickie stared at their mom.

"Not all of them." Astro sneered and leaned forward again. This time, he stared at Nickie, making her feel like a bucket of slugs had just been dumped down the back of her shirt. "What's your *idea*?"

"Laura left us a note." Nickie reached hesitantly into her back pocket. "We know what most of it means, but we—"

"How did you know there were three of us?" Emily asked.

"Em, come on."

"Seriously. We've never met you, and I'm almost positive Mom hasn't been here or talked or you since before we were born." Emily laced her fingers together and draped one arm over the high back of the armchair. "No one said there were three of us. How do you know that?"

Astro sucked his teeth, his frail body caving in on itself as he leaned even farther forward. His dark shirt, at least three sizes too big, hanging from his narrow shoulders. "You the one who likes to make trouble?"

Emily snorted but didn't look away. "When it's more trouble not to say or do anything? Yeah. That's me."

Nancy closed her eyes and sighed in defeat. Nickie was about to ask what was going on, but then Astro kicked against the floor and launched himself back in his chair, cackling. Huge brown loafers at the end of rail-thin legs pumped up and down, forcing the front legs of the armchair off the ground by at least an inch before they thumped back down onto the floor.

Emily fought back a laugh. The smoke—even most cleared by the fan in this room—made Nickie's eyes water.

"This is serious," Nancy said, using her stern voice on the old man throwing a fit of laughter in the armchair instead of her daughters this time. "I wouldn't have come here if we didn't need your help. You're the only person who—"

"I know who I am!" Astro thumped his cane onto the floor again with a loud crack. The thin smoke wafting lazily around the room burst away from him in a ripple of unseen energy, and he pulled himself to his feet. Despite being just under five feet tall, he commanded every inch of the room. "First, I will answer Emily's question because she answered mine."

"I asked first," Emily muttered.

Nickie kicked out behind the chair and knocked her boot against her sister's calf.

"*You* know how to see without seeing." Astro poked a finger in Emily's direction, then settled his hand on top of the cane again. "That's how I know about your sister Laura. I have seen each one of you before. In the haze." He spread his fingers over the cane and wiggled them frantically.

"So, what? You're, like, a soothsayer? An oracle?" Emily cocked her head. "Fortune-tell—"

"Ha! It's never a *fortune*, I can tell you that. I see, and then I unsee, and somewhere in between is everything else." Astro shuffled away from the armchairs toward the wall-length shelf at the back of his study. The smoke had almost cleared completely, and the Hadstrom sisters found themselves staring at an innocuous room in the odd man's house—except for the giant marble basin in front of the bookshelf, its unknown contents boiling and churning without being lit by any kind of heat. Thick bubbles burst at the surface, releasing more of the pungent smoke, which dissipated quickly instead of building up in another cloud to fill the study again.

Astro wagged a finger at Nancy and her daughters without looking at them. Emily wanted to shout at him to just tell her what to get for him. He moved about a foot a minute. "I know what you want from me. It's what everybody wants in one form or another. But you, I can show the future you're so curious to see."

"The future," Nickie repeated.

The old man cocked his head and gazed sideways at the ceiling. "Haven't heard an echo in here in decades."

Nancy rolled her eyes and stood. "I brought them here because they want to know—"

"Five years? Ten?" Astro dragged himself across the floor, studying the titles on his bookshelf from behind his ridiculously thick glasses.

"No, they called me about the—"

"I might not be able to see much farther than fifteen these days. You know, since the magic in this town broke apart like a loaf of bread set on by a nest of *rats.*"

"They want to know about the Tenebantur!" Nancy shouted, her hands balled into fists at her sides.

Astro stopped in his tracks, his shoulders hunched over the cane. Emily and Nickie stared at their mom, then exchanged glances. Nancy Milton didn't yell, and she didn't lose her cool.

The old man's joints creaked when he turned back to the women in his study. "You never told them who I am, but you told them about that, huh? Just throwing the words around like confetti? You know *so* much better than that, Nancy."

"I didn't tell them." Nancy's voice was hard and controlled and restrained now—a combination that meant the fury was being bottled up and saved for later. "Laura must have found it on her own and made the connection because she wrote it down for her sisters to find so they could use it to save her."

"Huh."

"And even if I told them, Astro, the information by itself is useless. I still would have brought Nickie and Emily here because you're the only one who can give them what they need."

Astro's huge eyes narrowed so much that Emily thought he'd closed them and drifted off to sleep standing in front of them. "Mom," she whispered. "What's going on?"

"Yes!" All three of the old man's guests jumped at his sudden exclamation. "What *is* this? How do three young witches know anything about the thing I created over two hundred years ago?"

"Two *hundred*?" Nickie slid her hand off the back of the armchair. "You've been around that long."

"Much longer. And I don't look a day over one-fifty. I know." Astro wheezed out another laugh and thumped his cane on the floor a few more times. His mirth stopped just as abruptly, and he grunted. "Why do you want the Tenebantur?"

"Because Laura wrote it down in a note she left us," Nickie muttered.

"What are you going to use it for, eh? I don't just give away these dangerous secrets for anyone. Not to mention that I'm running seriously low on supplies." Astro chuckled, which turned into another round of coughing.

"Whatever it is," Emily said, "we need it to help our sister. If you're really a soothsayer, did you see what happened to her last night?"

"I haven't seen anything for the last seven days, and it's killing me. Not literally, of course." Astro spread his arms and gestured to himself. "But it's killing me."

"That's our fault," Nickie said.

"Eh?"

"He doesn't know." Emily peered around the armchair to look at her mom. "He doesn't know about any of this."

"I may be senile, but I'm not deaf!"

"Gently, Em," Nickie whispered. "Don't give him a heart attack."

Astro pursed his lips in mocking fear and clutched his hands under his chin, blinking furiously. "Yes, please be gentle."

The fact that the guy just wasn't catching on to how important this was got under Emily's skin then, fueled by the childish whine in his voice. She stepped away from the armchair and headed toward him. "There's a gorafrex on this ship that's been locked up since the very beginning of the voyage. It escaped. Our family has been responsible for keeping it locked up, but it broke into our house last night and kidnapped our sister. It's going to kill her and use her for blood magic to power another energy core in a Velikan escape pod under Austin. If it does that, magic is *never* coming back, we will *never* see our sister again, and that escape pod will probably blow a massive hole in this ship and take all the passengers with it. Everyone. So we came to ask you about the Tenebantur, because that might be the only thing that'll stop that entire list of really bad things from happening. Apparently, you're the only person who knows what it is or can tell us so we can use it for whatever." When she stopped her rant, she was standing in front of Astro, towering over him despite being relatively short.

The ancient man squinted up at her, his wrinkled lips twitching into a sneer. "Tell me one more time why I should help you?"

Emily rolled her eyes. "Because I like to make trouble, and if you don't, I'll take your cane."

"*Emily*," Nancy whispered harshly.

Astro's tongue flickered across his crooked teeth, then he shook his cane at the youngest Hadstrom witch and cackled. "You certainly *make* me want to be terrified. But I do believe that you'll take my cane just because you're not supposed to snatch an old person's walking stick. Ha!"

"Thanks."

"Sure. Take it as a compliment." The man resumed his agonizingly slow pace toward the bookshelf. When he reached it, he moved his gnarled hand along the spines of many books, mumbling and shaking his head. "I invented the Tenebantur, you know. A fantastically perilous creation. And some of the elders, at least those in Austin, deemed it too destructive for common knowledge. Stuck it on the list with all the banned books they don't let you take to school these days."

"Like, banned magic books?"

"Like, banned knowledge in all its forms." Astro sniffed and searched through his books again. "But a few magicals in the area still know about it. How powerful it was. How much fun we had sitting around and scheming up all the ways we'd get to use it someday. Which, of course, will never happen."

Emily turned around to give her mom a questioning glance. Nancy just gestured toward the old soothsayer and sighed, clearly just as annoyed that he was taking so long.

"So, what is it?"

"It's a potion."

CHAPTER TWENTY-NINE

"You're kidding."

"It would be humiliating if I were, wouldn't it?" Astro chuckled, scanned a few more titles, then slammed his cane into the floor. "Where is it?"

"The Tenebantur is a potion?" Nickie stepped up beside her mother and whispered, "You couldn't have just told us that?"

"I've been making potions for days." Emily threw her arms out and let them slap back down against her thighs. "I had *Chuck* making potions. We don't have time to sit down and put together another one that the old dude made up two hundred years ago."

"Yes, very accurate description." Astro scoffed. "I made it up."

Emily shook her head in warning and eyed his cane. "What does it do?"

"To put it bluntly, you little troublemaker, it's a trap."

"What?"

Astro scratched his head and growled in frustration at

whatever he couldn't find on his bookshelf. "You know what a trap is. Don't play dumb. Innocuous at first. Doesn't look like much. Doesn't give much of a warning. Then an unsuspecting magical tries to deactivate it or even walk right through it if they're not paying attention, and *bam!*" He thumped his cane again. "Instant disaster."

"For the magical who doesn't know how to counteract it?" Nickie asked.

"For everyone, most likely." Astro shrugged. "I've only been able to use it once, and oh, that was a beautiful explosion. You could see it for hundreds of miles. Turned the sky green."

"I'm not sure that's what we need." Emily glanced at her mom and sister, trying to find the right words to get through to the crazy old man. "We don't want to blow up the gorafrex. I mean, we do, but not like that. Not when it could hurt so many people. And not while that thing still has Laura."

"Who said anything about *you* using the Tenebantur?" Astro tsked at her and frowned beneath thin, barely existent white eyebrows. "You almost had me convinced you were smart."

"Then I give up." Emily turned away from him and headed back toward the house's entrance. "Come on, Nickie. We'll figure it out some other way."

"No, you will *not!*" When Astro thumped his cane again, a cold draft burst across the study and sent a shiver up Emily's spine. "Any other way will get you killed."

"Just give it to them," Nancy said. "I'll pay for it."

"Oh!" The soothsayer tittered and scrunched his face even more. "What an excellent idea."

"What do you want?"

"One hour, two days a week for the next year. And you pay for all the supplies, you understand? I'm not in the habit of leaving my home unless it's been burned to the ground."

Nancy spread her arms and nodded. "Fine."

"Yes, it is." Astro grinned, then jumped when he remembered what he'd been looking for. "And so is this." His aged hand reached up to pluck two strands of what was left of his wiry silver hair. Then he leaned over his cane and wiggled the hairs at the Hadstrom sisters. "Who wants it?"

"Tempting, really," Emily muttered.

Nickie stepped forward and opened her hand so the man could set his hair in her palm. "What's this for?"

"For tearing down the Tenebantur." Astro nodded vigorously. "You put *that* in any option you like and use it when you need it. That is the only way to avoid killing yourselves."

"Awesome." Nickie started to turn toward her sister to hand over the old-man hair, but Emily beat her to it.

"I got it. Just hold still." Emily pulled a vial from a pocket of her vest and uncorked it. "I have a feeling we won't be getting any more of these if something happens." Behind her, Astro snorted. Emily carefully lifted the hairs from her sister's palm and lowered them into the potion. Bright orange liquid deepened into a muddy brown for a few seconds before resuming its previous color.

"Em."

"Yeah."

"What potion did you just put those into?"

Emily shrugged and pocketed the vial again. "A good one. Trust me."

Nickie watched her sister's hand pat the pocket she thought Emily had said was for the explosives. *Now is not the right time to bring that up.*

"Okay." Emily pressed her hands together and faced Astro for a little bow, which could have been entirely sincere or the youngest Hadstrom witch's version of sarcastic gratitude. "Nice to meet you, Soothsayer. I hope we never have to do this again."

"You and me both, witch."

With a final nod at the old man, Emily made her way toward the entrance of Astro's house and gestured for Nickie to join her. "You comin', Mom?"

"Yep. I'm right behind you." But Nancy stayed for just a little longer, listening to her daughters step out into the hall and open the front door on their own. Astro wiggled his eyebrows at her but didn't say another word. "I'll be here on Friday."

"What? Don't you have a life? You should be out living it on a Friday night."

Nancy pressed her lips together and dipped her head toward the soothsayer. "And twice a week for a year. You might wanna work on your speed, old man. I'm a lot faster than I used to be."

"I have no doubt." Astro brushed his fingers toward the house's entryway and smacked his lips. "Now get out of my house."

She didn't let herself smile until she felt the cold, heavy mist of the soothsayer's smoke close in behind her, then she followed her daughters out onto the rotting front porch and firmly closed the door.

Nickie and Emily faced her on the cement walkway, their arms folded, with mirrored expressions of curiosity and blame. "I think now's the part where you explain how the heck you know a soothsayer."

Emily glanced at her sister and shrugged. "What she said."

"Keep walking." Nancy spread her arms and ushered her daughters down the path toward their cars at the curb. "I know Astro from a long time ago. From before I knew your dad, actually."

"I asked how, Mom. Not when."

"He used to be my mentor."

"Your…"

Emily's eyes grew wide. "Like, you were his *apprentice*?"

Nancy shrugged. "That's old-school, Em, but yeah. It's basically the same thing."

"No way."

"He's one of the best potionsmasters in the US and one of maybe four soothsayers on the entire continent. I was lucky enough to get his attention, and eventually, I got to learn from him too."

Nickie wrinkled her nose. "How did you get his attention?"

Their mom rested a hand on each of their shoulders and blinked at the street. "By blowing things up."

Emily's mouth dropped open. Nickie froze.

Having stunned both her daughters into silence, Nancy stepped between them off the sidewalk and headed for her car. "I'm guessing you have everything you need at this point. If Laura mentioned the Tenebantur, you're good to go. So go. And I love you."

"Love you too, Mom," Nickie muttered, finally looking up to watch her mom slip behind the wheel of her Camry.

"Blowing things up?" Emily blinked, then absently raised her hand and waved as Nancy drove down the street. "And she paid for two soothsayer hairs with an hour twice a week for a year. Of doing *what?*"

"I have no idea, Em." Nickie stepped around the front of her car and opened the driver's side door. "That can wait until after we get Laura. Then she can speculate all she wants about what Mom got herself into way back when."

"Right." Forcing herself to focus on the most important thing right now, Emily opened the passenger side door and slipped into the seat. "Okay. We're stocked up like a CVS before Halloween. With potions and weapons, not candy."

Nickie ignored the weirdness of that statement. "Which energy core are we gonna check out first?"

"We don't have the time to go to both, do we?" Emily pointed at one pocket of her fishing vest, reconsidered, and reached into the one beside it. She drew out the vial with the dropperful of iron-enhanced tracking potion and twisted it open. "No twitching away from me this time, okay?"

Nickie smirked and held out her ring. "If you hurry up before the gorafrex has a chance to try using magic again and blasting drums into my brain, sure."

Shaking her head, Emily carefully lowered the dropper toward Nickie's black legacy ring and squeezed out just one drop. The ring flashed silver, then black before the drop of potion disappeared.

"Woah." Nickie drew back her hand and twisted it back and forth. "Tingles."

"Woohoo." Emily paused with the drop over her copper legacy ring and glanced into the back seat. "Wanna pick up your amp? Maybe grab the daggers out of the glovebox?"

"And drive all the way to the last energy core when this potion starts tracking Laura? I don't think that's gonna be very helpful, Em."

"I'm just trying to cover our bases, okay? I don't know how powerful this potion is or exactly *how* it's going to track Laura's ring. It could be just like the singing bowl, or it could be like your Clubhouse coin today and whisk us off to who knows where. And I do *not* want us to show up unannounced without all of our gear."

Nickie blinked at her sister, then took a sharp breath. "Excellent point." She reached into the back and grabbed her portable amp, put it in her lap, and leaned across Emily's legs to grab both wickedly sharp iron daggers from the glovebox. "You get one."

"Totally."

"And if this potion doesn't teleport us both, these blades are going right back in there. I'm not driving and waving a huge knife at the same time."

"I wouldn't expect you to."

"Okay."

Emily settled the iron orb and the dagger on her lap, then brought the dropper of thick silver potion over her copper ring and squeezed out one more drop. Her ring flashed silver and copper too, then the drop disappeared. "Tingles? More like slipped it off the stove and right onto my finger."

"Or that." Nickie licked her lips and stared at her ring. "So, how long until this thing tracking potion kicks—"

The world lurched around the Hadstrom sisters, tumbling end over end and jerking them in every direction all at once. Emily thought she shouted something, but she couldn't tell over the debilitating feeling of being ripped apart.

When the world stopped again, she dropped a few feet and landed on her backside in the dirt. It knocked the wind out of her, and she braced herself with a hand against the ground before she had the chance to fall over.

Nickie landed beside her with a grunt. Her guitar strings brushed the portable amp and twanged as it toppled out of her lap and on its side in the dirt. "That was the *worst* way to get anywhere quickly."

"Yeah, I'm missing the transport bubbles right now." Grimacing, Emily pushed herself onto her knees and looked around. "Nickie."

"I'm okay, Em. I mean, my head hurts, but—"

Emily lunged sideways and clamped a hand over her sister's mouth, shushing her. Nickie stared at her with wide eyes, and when the youngest Hadstrom sister pointed through the woods just in front of where they'd landed, Nickie shuddered.

About a dozen yards away, the air shimmered between the trees, oscillating between perfectly clear and a milky-white haze like soap bubbles. Beyond that was the rest of the forest—huge live oaks, a blackberry thicket, and the tweeting of birds venturing out to test the dropping heat of early afternoon. The shimmering wall of the gorafrex's

Tenebantur spread in both directions as far as either Hadstrom sister could see.

"We're here," Emily whispered and slowly removed her hand from Nickie's mouth.

"Ready?"

"Oh, yeah."

CHAPTER THIRTY

As quietly as they could, Nickie and Emily stood and did a quick inventory of what they'd brought with them. Nickie gave her sister a thumbs-up, and Emily nodded. They moved through the trees, watching and waiting for whatever might pop out at them.

The gorafrex is on the other side of that warded wall, and it has Laura. Emily flexed her fingers inside the half-fingered glove her oldest sister had made her. *That monster could try anything.*

Nickie uncoiled the cable from the top of her amp and plugged it into her Strat, although she left the power off until she needed to use her music.

When they were six feet away from the wall, a high-pitched buzz filled the air. It was so quiet, Nickie thought she was starting to get another migraine, but it didn't get any louder, and the migraine didn't come. Emily cocked her head and pointed to her ear. Her sister nodded.

With a shrug, Emily reached into the bottom-right pocket of her vest and drew out the vial of bright-orange potion plus soothsayer's hair. She wiggled it in front of Nickie, then mouthed, 'Stand back.'

Nickie didn't hesitate, and Emily turned to the right before taking aim at the shimmering wall in front of them. She drew her arm back, took a deep breath, and chucked the vial as hard as she could at what looked like a bubble.

A bright orange stain appeared on the wall, sending crackling streaks of orange light through the trees. The magical wall blinked a few times, like it had shorted out, and Emily stuck a hand on her hip. "I thought—"

The wards exploded with blinding light and heat and force, sending a shockwave of all three in every direction. It knocked both Hadstrom sisters off their feet and tossed them through the woods. Trees splintered and toppled all around them. Emily landed painfully on her side. She thought she cried out but couldn't hear anything beyond the rushing in her ears and the thunderous roar of what she had just blown up. Twigs and leaves and small stones pelted the sisters for longer than should have been possible, stinging Nickie's back as she hunched over in the fallen leaves and covered her head.

Then everything fell still again. "Nickie?" Emily groaned and pushed herself up slowly. "You okay?"

"What?"

"Are you okay?"

"Probably." Nickie blinked hard and shook her head. "That was…"

"That was awesome." Emily winced and stuck a finger in her ear to try wiggling the ringing out of it. Then she looked past the warded wall of Tenebantur that no longer existed. "Good thing we don't have to be quiet anymore."

"There's no way that thing doesn't know we're here." Nickie pushed to her feet and brushed the leaves and twigs off her guitar. She carefully pulled a much larger branch out of the sound hole, tossed it aside, and picked up her amp again. "So let's hurry."

"Huh?"

"Let's go!"

Emily stood and looked around for her iron orb. When she found it and bent over to pick it up, the feeling of her wet shirt against her ribs made her stop. "Oh, no."

"What?"

"I think..." Emily reached tentatively into her vest pocket and pulled out shards of broken glass dripping purple glowing liquid. She tossed them behind her and wiped her fingers on her pants. "We lost a potion."

"Em, please tell me it wasn't a super-important one."

"They're all important. Come on." Emily nodded at the center of the clearing that had been revealed by the explosion. The gorafrex's Tenebantur had hidden the entrance to a small cave, which was now a dark, cold hole in front of them.

"Right. Just go storming into the gorafrex's cave. That's our plan."

"It's better than no plan. And now we know they're here. Hurry up."

They reached the entrance and peered into the darkness. Emily grabbed Nickie's shoulder and quickly summoned an orb of light from her copper ring. She waved it in front of them, and the orb lit up a natural series of stone steps heading steeply underground. "We're coming," Nickie whispered, and they stepped inside.

The cold was overpowering, especially after the humid heat of the forest behind them. The sisters descended as quickly as they could while trying not to slip on the slick rock. The stairs stretched on seemingly forever, then a flash of silver light spilled toward them from the cavern at the bottom.

A woman's high, agonized scream tore through the cavern and the tunnel and up the stairs. "No." Emily took off running toward the sound, her sneakers sliding on the stone worn smooth by centuries of water dripping from somewhere.

"Laura!" Nickie shouted, close on her sister's heels. "We're coming!"

It would have been impossible for anyone to hear their shouts over the endless scream. When it stopped, it was only for half a second before it started up again. "Come on, come on!" Emily darted down the last few steps and barreled through the passage toward the strobing silver light and the screams. She fished around in her pocket for another explosive potion, deciding she would much rather toss this at the gorafrex and heal its human host later than hesitate and risk Laura's screams dying out forever.

Nickie jerked the power knob on the side of her amp, which let out its own scream until she adjusted the volume. Emily jumped at the sound and crashed into the tunnel wall but kept moving. "Laura!"

Finally, they reached the chamber at the end of the passage. Emily skidded to a stop and drew her arm back to take aim with her potion vial. Nickie bumped into her when she stopped, squaring her feet and dropping the amp just before she strummed the first deafening chord of the song that brought the gorafrex to its knees every time.

Only the gorafrex's human host—a woman they hadn't yet had the misfortune of meeting—was already on her knees. And the scream that just wouldn't stop came not from Laura's mouth but from the possessed Peabrain.

"What the—" Emily's mouth fell open as she took in the energy core rising from its metal cradle on the floor to the ceiling. The gorafrex was pressed flat against the clear glass-like material of the column, both hands wrapped tightly around a bright silver pole digging into its chest. The other end of the iron lance was firmly clasped in Laura Hadstrom's hands, and she leaned against it with all her might, her feet propped against a boulder rising from the chamber floor.

On the other side of their sister, Leonidas, the fairy owner of Brightwing Emporium, stared at their expected rescuers with intense urgency.

Laura turned her head just enough to shoot her sisters a grin of fierce determination and a little relief. "Took you long enough."

Emily darted into the chamber. "Obviously, our timing was perfect."

The gorafrex screamed again and struggled against the lance pinning it to the energy core. Leonidas jumped, then stripped the ropes off his wrists and chucked them at the ground. "I'm assuming the three of you know what to do," he shouted.

"This is it," Laura said. "The rune has it now. We just need your separation potion, Em."

Emily's hand passed over the wet stain on her vest, and

the minute she glanced at Nickie, the middle Hadstrom sister whipped the guitar strap over her head and set everything down.

"That's the one that broke?"

"Yeah."

"What do we do now?"

Laura grunted and put more weight behind the lance digging into the gorafrex's chest. "I can't hold this forever."

"I *know*." Emily closed her eyes and clenched her fists. "We need… We need something to—"

"We need that potion, Emily." The gorafrex struggled against Laura's lance again and almost managed to push itself away from the energy core. Laura screamed back at it, and Nickie grabbed the end of the lance to add her weight to it.

"Release me!" the gorafrex roared, whipping its host's head back and forth and tearing at the end of the lance like it thought humans suddenly had claws.

"Not even if you asked nicely." Emily paced across the chamber as her sisters held the unleashed creature at bay.

"Emily?"

"I'm thinking!"

Laura's chest heaved as she pushed against her iron weapon. "Think faster, Em. Like, a lot faster than it took you to get here."

Emily shouted in surprise and whirled to face her sisters. "That's it." She tore at the pocket of her vest where she'd returned the tracking potion with the piece of the Isolation Vein. "For all the parts of a whole."

"You don't have to explain, Em. Just do it."

"Yeah. Yeah, okay. Laura, where are your keys?"

"Oh." Leonidas darted forward and almost crashed to his knees when he stooped to pick up Laura's keyring from the floor. "Here."

"Thanks. Nickie?"

"Back pocket, Em. Always."

Emily darted toward her sister and pulled Nickie's keys from her pocket. Then she pulled out her own and clenched all three keyrings in one hand. "I need some extra hands."

Leonidas didn't say a word as he rushed to her side and cupped both hands in front of him.

Deep, rolling laughter like stones crumbling against each other filled the chamber. "You're out of options," the gorafrex seethed, jerking fruitlessly against the lance. "Nothing but empty hopes for an accidental victory. I've spent centuries waiting. You don't think that's enough time to learn everything there is to know about how useless your magic is?"

"Ignore it, Em." Nickie pushed harder against the lance.

"That's the plan." Emily sifted through the keys and dropped two of them into Leonidas' outstretched hands. "Don't move." Then she pulled the dropper out of the vial and squirted the silver potion on one Clubhouse coin, then the second. "Don't touch that part."

Leonidas jerked his head up to stare at her. "Wasn't planning on it."

The gorafrex bucked, snarling and whipping the woman's head around as her shoes slipped on the stone floor, trying to gain traction. "You cannot hold me here like this forever."

"Just a little longer." Emily dropped the potion on the

third Clubhouse coin, then had to dip the dropper back into the vial to get more.

"I'll take all your magic before this is finished," the gorafrex screamed. "Every last bit of it. And instead of using just one of you, I'll have blood magic from three *Hadstroms* like I should've taken in the beginning."

"Shut up!" Emily's hand darted toward the lance in her sisters' hands.

The gorafrex shoved at the lance with surprising force and took them all off-guard when it tried to slip out of its host's body. Its primal drumbeat burst through the cavern, bringing down huge chunks of rock from the ceiling.

Nickie cried out and doubled over. Her hands slipped from the lance just as Emily squeezed the last of the potion onto the bright iron. Laura shouted in surprise when Nickie's reinforcement suddenly disappeared. The gorafrex shuddered and glowed with the wavering aura as it pulled itself from the human woman unwillingly lending it her body. Emily leapt forward and grabbed the lance before driving it as hard as she could into the gorafrex's chest.

A hollow thud reverberated up the column of the energy core, inhuman laughter spilled from the human host's open mouth, and then the cackling creature disappeared. Emily flew forward and fell to her knees when the tip of the lance hit the glass-like column with a shrill ping.

"Ow!" Leonidas dropped the keyrings on the floor and shook out his hands. "What kind of irresponsible idiot makes a—"

He stopped at the earsplitting crack coming from the energy core. Blue and green lines snaked their way up the clear column, and the chamber rumbled with the threat of collapsing on top of them. "Get out!" Emily snatched up the lance and tossed it at Laura, who almost fell forward, trying to catch it.

Nickie forced herself through the pain in her head and grabbed the keyrings off the floor. The Hadstrom sisters stumbled out of the energy core chamber, Leonidas following, his pale blue wings fluttering behind him.

With an echoing crack, the energy core shattered and split in every direction, throwing broken shards against the stone walls. A roar like jet engines firing up shook the chamber and the passage and the stairs, and everything that wasn't tied down to the stone lifted off the ground and hovered.

The Hadstrom witches pulled themselves along the passage walls and up the stairs, gravity lost while the urgency remained to get out of there. Laura opened her mouth to shout something, but no sound came out.

The party scrambled along the walls, moving toward the dimming light spilling through the forest above them. Then the forces of nature fell back into place. The energy core exploded and sent a massive blast through the passage and the stairway, tossing the Hadstrom witches and their apothecary friend aboveground like a geyser spouting water. Green and blue light streaked from the cave's opening, bursting through the trees and lighting up the woods.

Just before the ground rushed up to meet them, light and sound and gravity returned. The last thing Nickie remembered was that she'd left her Strat and that brand-new red amp in the chamber.

CHAPTER THIRTY-ONE

Rubbing her head, Laura dropped to the forest floor to sit between her sisters. They stared at what remained of the cave—just a pile of rock now. They'd left Leonidas sprawled on the ground a few yards away because he'd told them he needed a minute to himself before he could join anyone else's conversation.

Finally, Emily broke the silence. "So. You guys think a Clubhouse in a different dimension counts as a gorafrex prison?"

Laura lowered her gaze to the three keyrings laid out on the grass in front of them. "Seeing as we have the only keys right here, I'd say that's a pretty strong maybe."

"Yeah, but the Peabrain's in there too. *With* the gorafrex." Nickie brushed a clump of dried mud off her knee. "We can't leave her in there like that."

"No, we can't." Laura took a deep breath. "So when we destroy the last energy core and set magic right again, we'll get her out. Whatever it takes. And we'll put that thing back where it belongs."

"We found the prison." Emily let out a wry chuckle. "I mean, the door, or whatever. Cut out a chunk of the iron that made it in the first place. And our rings."

Nickie leaned forward to shoot Emily a knowing glance. "I'm not sure 'cut it out' is the right term, Em."

"You know what I mean."

"That's how you found me?" Laura asked.

"Yeah. That and your clever jellyfish clue." Emily patted the almost-empty pockets of her vest. "Same potion that sucked the gorafrex into the Clubhouse."

Laura patted her youngest sister's thigh and nodded. "The rune bound it to the lance, and you transferred all that to our keyring coins with the tracking potion. That was really quick thinking, Em."

"Oh, yeah? You know, for some reason, I got the distinct impression that you wanted me to think faster."

The sisters shared a weary laugh.

"Hey, did you have a plan for what you'd do after you'd pinned the gorafrex against the energy core with your pointy iron stick?" Nickie bumped her shoulder against Laura's. "Like a Plan B, in case we didn't show up?"

"Absolutely not. I always count on you two showing up. We just got lucky with the timing."

Emily stuck out her foot and nudged the lance lying in the grass. "How the heck did you get this thing out of the Clubhouse?"

"Again, lucky with the timing." Laura stared at the iron tool that had probably saved all their lives. "My keyring worked, I took advantage of it, and when magic dumped me back into the chamber, *boom*. You guys blew up the Tenebantur. Perfect distraction."

"Do you have *any* idea what a Tenebantur is?"

Laura looked over her shoulder at Leonidas, who hadn't moved an inch but let out a deep sigh. "Only what our fairy friend told me about it. I think he knew the guy who invented it."

"You won't believe this." Emily chuckled and dragged her hands down the sides of her face. "So do we."

"So does Mom," Nickie added.

The oldest Hadstrom witch stared at each of her sisters in turn. "I'm gone for less than twenty-four hours, and you two suddenly know everything I don't."

"Not something we should try again." Emily closed her eyes. "Like, ever."

"I second that."

"Well, I'm not *planning* to get kidnapped again, so we can all agree on that one."

"Nickie?"

"Yeah, Em."

"Sorry about your guitar."

"Yeah. Me too. Wasn't a magic guitar, though. I can get another one."

"And I need to get shatter-proof pockets." Emily smoothed a hand down her fishing vest and shook her head. "Trial and error, right?"

"You have any potions to take us home?" Laura nodded at Emily's vest.

"Nope. Lost those somewhere in the exploding energy core and no gravity bits." Emily grabbed Laura's knee and nodded at Nickie, who did the same. "Pretty sure we can get back almost as quickly, though. Especially now that we have you backing us up, Dr. Hadstrom."

Laura rolled her eyes. "Magic's only been getting worse, Em. You can try if you want, but I don't think you're gonna get a transport bubble anytime soon."

All three legacy rings flashed on the Hadstrom sisters' thumbs, and Nickie's black ring produced a bright yellow bubble that grew in front of them until it was the right size to fit all of them inside. Laura coughed. "How did you…"

Nickie grinned. "We have a lot to tell you."

"That's an understatement."

As the witches stood in front of the transport bubble—probably the only one in all of Austin at that point—Emily leaned toward the apothecary owner and shouted, "Leonidas! Want a ride?"

The fairy pushed himself up on his elbows and opened his mouth for a witty reply. When he saw the transport bubble, the only thing he could think of to say was, "Does it work?"

Emily snorted and shot her sisters a knowing glance. "Does it work? Can you believe this guy?"

The End

The sisters are starting to figure things out and are getting better at working together. Will it be enough? Find out in *Magic Underground!*

Get sneak peeks, exclusive giveaways, behind the scenes content, and more.
PLUS you'll be notified of special **one day only fan pricing** on new releases.

Sign up today to get free stories.

CLICK HERE

or visit: https://marthacarr.com/read-free-stories/

I've been in the writing game as a journalist and columnist and author for over thirty years and have interacted with a lot of editors. A good one will easily lift your words to a better place without losing the writer's voice. That is harder than it looks. It requires the editor to put aside their own writerly ideas and live within the author's intent, their way of saying something and wanting to make that better. And when a writer finds a good one, we cultivate that relationship that's just like a friendship. There's so much that can be learned about a writer's personality by really looking at what they write...

Judah Raine is a great editor. She comes in so gently and fixes the places that need to be fixed to make the entire book read more easily and let the reader get sucked into the action and the relationships. But the footprint is still the author's and it's as if she knows just what stones to turn this way or that without disturbing the design. Trust me, editing is an art form as well and the best ones like Judah are a kind of Picasso behind the scenes.

Martha Carr

1. What turns you on?

Life and everything there is to learn, even the little snippets of 'useless' information that seem to have no relevance but are simply so frigging fun.

2. What turns you off?

People who don't want to learn or won't continually push to improve.

3. Who do you most admire? Why?

Nelson Mandela, because he truly was a man to respect for his wisdom, forgiveness, and vision. Second, Jannie Smuts, because he was a simple farm boy who grew into a vision to change the way people interacted.

4. What profession other than your own would you like to attempt?

Lol, honestly? I've tried a few in my...let's call it an interesting...life. I'm in the profession I was made for—writing and editing—but if I had to choose to give something a whirl... IT – you know, all those sneaky, complicated, cyber-language stuff that gets you into places you shouldn't go. Hacking? Is that what they call it? Oh...

5. What profession would you not like to do?

Chef or anything cooking related. EVER.

6. If heaven exists, what would you like to hear God say when you arrive at the pearly gates?

"I have a surprise for you."

7. What is your favorite movie?

Not fair. Favorite as in "that was so much fun?" I guess for the laughter factor my all-time best would be A Fish Called Wanda. Not a popular choice, I know, but it appeals to the crazy in me and still today, I laugh fit to bust. (And I believe in laughing.) Serious movies? Schindler's List made a huge impression on me that nothing I've seen since, (and there have been many), will ever compare. Rugged, raw, uncluttered, and real. Then there's... okay, enough.

8. Who is your favorite character and from what book by which author?

Uh...all of them? It's like asking me to choose which of my children I love more.

9. What is something most people do not know about you?

I hate gunky hands. This is the girl who washes her hands each time she peels a potato. Oh, and I'm a Cat Person.

10. What do you look forward to most in the new year?

Meh, I'm not much of a new year kind of girl, honestly. Today is what matters. Each day is new. It's a chance to do something new, something more, something better than yesterday. I suppose I live the eternal "new year" starting every single day. When you've almost died a few times, your perspective changes.

11. What's your favorite non-LMBPN series you've done? What's your favorite series inside LMBPN?

The Zoooooo!!!

Other series in the Terranavis Universe:

The Adventures of Maggie Parker
The Adventures of Finnegan Dragonbender

If you enjoyed this series, you may enjoy these series in the Oriceran Universe:

THE LEIRA CHRONICLES
I FEAR NO EVIL
REWRITING JUSTICE
SCHOOL OF NECESSARY MAGIC
SCHOOL OF NECESSARY MAGIC: RAINE CAMPBELL
ALISON BROWNSTONE
THE DANIEL CODEX SERIES
FEDERAL AGENTS OF MAGIC
SCIONS OF MAGIC
THE UNBELIEVABLE MR. BROWNSTONE
THE KACY CHRONICLES

MIDWEST MAGIC CHRONICLES
SOUL STONE MAGE
THE FAIRHAVEN CHRONICLES

OTHER BOOKS BY JUDITH BERENS

OTHER BOOKS BY MARTHA CARR

OTHER BOOKS BY MICHAEL ANDERLE

JOIN THE TERRANAVIS UNIVERSE FAN GROUP ON FACEBOOK!